MORTIMER

The Leader Within

ANTHONY WILSON

Copyright © 2013 by Anthony Wilson

All rights reserved. Published in the United States by Anthony Wilson, Rochester, Minnesota

Copyediting by Ricki Walters. www.rlweditorial.com

Cover design and artwork by Karri Klawiter. www.artbykarri.com

ISBN 978-0-9895437-0-5 (Paperback)
ISBN 978-0-9895437-2-9 (eBook)

For Mom and Dad, who molded.
For Linda Rae, who enriches.
For Ky and Jo, who inspire.

Acknowledgements

I learned a few lessons while writing *Mortimer*. Most importantly, you can't do this kind of thing alone. Fortunately, I had a lot of people willing to help.

Thank you to my review group for helping transform early drafts into something that actually made sense: Sara Farmer, Natalie Grimm, Regi Herges, Sandy Jensen, Toby Jensen, Danni Kimzey, Paul Kimzey, Emily Lundt, Val Lukas, Jason Wampfler, Jordyn Wilson, Kyler Wilson and Linda Wilson.

To Martin Gibbs, I appreciate your input and guidance as I navigated the publishing process.

To my family and friends, many of you influenced the characters and storylines that appear on the following pages.

Finally, to the reader, without you this whole effort would be pointless. Maybe someone recommended this book. Maybe you just stumbled across it. Maybe I begged you to read it. Regardless, thanks for giving *Mortimer* a chance. I hope you enjoy the adventure.

Anthony Wilson

MORTIMER
The Leader Within

PROLOUGE

Nap time was not working out as planned. Jimmy had promised that he would go to sleep if his mom and dad let him lie down in the living room instead of the upstairs bedroom. He was trying, but the sofa felt funny. It wasn't as soft as usual and it didn't smell right.

The people outside were making a lot of noise. The six-year-old flipped himself over and peeked out the window. There weren't as many trucks and vans as before, but there were still a bunch of them. And there were a lot of people standing around, talking on their phones, looking through their cameras. It was because of his Papa. Papa was a very important man. Everyone liked Papa. They were sad that he had died. Jimmy was sad too.

A sudden clanking noise on the porch startled Jimmy. He crawled off of the sofa and slowly moved closer to the window. The flag that his dad had hung by the steps was twisting in the wind. The pole was banging against the rain gutter. Jimmy could see that it had slipped out of its holder. The flag was drooping toward the ground. He needed to fix it. Papa had always told him that a flag should never touch the ground.

Jimmy moved toward the door, twisted the lock and slowly turned the handle. He peered at the trucks, and vans, and people as the door opened. They had been there all day, ever since he and his mom and dad and Nana had gotten back from the cemetery. There had been a lot more trucks and vans at the cemetery. Lots more people, too. When he rode back to his Nana's house in the big black car, the trucks and vans and people had followed them. But they couldn't go past the gate, or on the driveway, or on the grass, because the police wouldn't let them. They had to stay on the street, or the sidewalk, in front of the fence.

The flag clanged again. It was going to fall.

Jimmy left the door open behind him as he moved across the porch toward the steps. He grabbed the flag and untwisted it from the pole, being very careful not to let it touch the porch or the steps. He reached high, slipped the flag pole back into the holder, and then pulled on the bottom of the flag to make sure it hung straight.

People were shouting at him from the street. He looked toward the trucks and vans. The people who had been talking on their phones and looking in their cameras were now all looking at him. He moved back toward the door and gasped when he felt himself being pulled upward.

"Didn't I tell you to stay inside?" It was his dad. He swung Jimmy around and whisked him back inside before Jimmy could take another breath.

"What were you doing out there?" snipped his dad, closing the door with his foot and lowering Jimmy back to the floor in front of him. He kept a hold on one of Jimmy's arms while he waited for an answer.

Jimmy could feel the tears coming. Dad was mad. He didn't get mad very often, but Jimmy didn't like it when it happened.

"What's all the commotion out here?" A voice came from down the hallway. Jimmy's Nana walked toward them drying her hands on a kitchen towel.

"He was outside on the porch," said his dad. "I told him to stay inside and away from the windows." His dad let go of his arm. He didn't seem to be as mad now.

"Where were you going JP?" asked Nana. Everyone called him Jimmy, except for his Nana. She always called him JP.

Jimmy looked at her, but didn't say anything.

"Answer your grandmother, son," said his dad.

Jimmy looked at the floor. "Nowhere."

The tears arrived. Jimmy turned and ran back into the living room. He jumped back onto the sofa and shoved his head under a stack of pillows. One of the pillows bounced onto the end table knocking a statue onto the floor, shattering it.

Jimmy quickly rose from under the pillows. It was one of Papa's birds, one of Papa's *favorite* birds. It was broken all over the floor. This was why he wasn't allowed to run in the house or jump on the furniture. Nana had always told him not to run and jump in the house.

Now the tears were really coming.

"Uh-oh," said Nana, moving toward the couch. "I don't think he's ever gonna fly again."

She put her arm around her grandson and held him as he sobbed. Jimmy buried himself between her and the pillows, trying to disappear.

"I'll get the broom," said his dad.

Jimmy cried for several minutes while his grandmother held him and scratched the top of his head. He loved it when Nana scratched his head. She would often snuggle with him on the sofa and scratch his head until he fell asleep. He also loved the way Nana smelled. She always smelled this way. This was how the sofa was supposed to smell too.

After a few minutes, Nana stretched him out, tucked a pillow under his arm, and covered him with a blanket.

"Sorry, Nana," Jimmy said as she rose from the sofa.

"It's OK, honey," she said. "Accidents happen."

"But it was Papa's favorite," said Jimmy.

"You were Papa's favorite," said Nana. "You don't need to worry about that bird. He had lots of birds."

CHAPTER 1

Wednesday, January 21, 2037

Hot steam filled the shower, as the water cascaded down his back. He breathed deeply, allowing himself to indulge a bit longer. The water and pressure felt good. He could definitely get used to this, but not today. He pressed the blue button on the control panel and held it as the indicator lights turned from bright red to blue. He silently counted to five as the powerful spray turned ice cold and jolted away the last remnants of slumber.

James Patrick Martin was now fully awake.

As the fog lifted, he worked an oversized towel through his hair, shaking out the final few cobwebs from a very short night of sleep. Uncharacteristically, they had stayed out until 2 a.m. and he did not get to bed until 2:30. He guessed it was now about 5:27. He would have to find a way to make up that extra 30 seconds of hot steamy bliss if he was still going to make it to the office before 6 a.m.

Stepping from the shower, he grabbed a robe from the nearby rack. Heated tiles warmed his feet. According to Rae, the heated floor was an "absolute must." He thought it was somewhat extravagant, but had decided not to argue. Rae had agreed to make all of the new housing arrangements, including the master bath. Based on his first shower in the new place, she had done an excellent job.

It was amazing how different things looked from when he had first seen the room a few weeks ago. The walls were in the same place, but that was about all that was left unchanged. New paint, new molding, and new fixtures had been added. The Jacuzzi was gone. The artwork on the walls was new, but very familiar. French Country style, landscapes and cottages, Rae's signature style for every bathroom they had ever shared. He moved toward the sink and vanity, stepping from the warm tiles onto a cozy woven rug. If nothing else, his feet were going to love this place.

While looking into the mirror, he worked his hair with the bath towel one last time and noted the scattered lines of grey that were showing up inside his short cut sideburns. Having just turned 51, a little spattering of grey was to be expected. Most of the men he knew, even the ones in their 40s, had some grey or had given in to color treatments. His natural look was still truly natural. His dark brown hair was parted on the right. He kept his bangs long so that a few strands would hang down onto his forehead. Rae called them "flippies," and she very much disliked it when they were trimmed away. His eyes were steel blue and had provided him with life-long perfect vision; no glasses, no contacts, and no lasers. All in all, he felt like he had aged gracefully, except for the soft belly that had taunted him since his college days.

As he reached for his hairbrush, he noticed a shiny round object next to the sink. At first glance, he thought it was quarter, but looking closer he saw a soaring eagle. No words. No date. He picked up the coin and turned it over to reveal several letters and numbers etched into the back.

OO.1.2

2:05 p.m.

He turned the coin over and looked at the eagle again, then flipped back to the etching. *OO.1.2* was totally meaningless to him. Even stranger was the fact that he was certain the coin was not on the vanity before he got in the shower. He knew because he had searched every inch of the bathroom looking for shaving cream before finding a can in the shower caddy, right where it should be, right where Rae had placed it.

There was a light knock on the door. He slipped the coin into the pocket of his robe and turned toward the door.

"Beware, boingy-haired wife coming through," said a sleepy-eyed Rae, clad in a silky robe.

She shuffled barefoot into the bathroom, eyes barely open. Her long brown hair was tousled and curled. "Ohhh...nice tiles," she said, slipping her arms around him and burying her face into his damp, but still plush, robe. "You love the tiles don't you? Say you love the tiles."

"I love the tiles," he said, kissing her on the top of the head. "What are you doing up? It's still pretty early."

"You think I'm going to let you have all the fun today?" she said, burrowing deeper into his robe.

"I guess not," he said, pushing her away just enough to allow him to gently kiss her forehead. "You're going to love that shower."

She opened one eye and smiled, "Point me in the right direction."

"I bet you can find it," he said, turning her around. "You designed the place."

"What do you think?" she asked, stepping toward the shower.

"I love it. Very comfortable."

Turning back toward the vanity and picking up the hairbrush, he hesitated. "Is this the first time you've been in here?"

"Do you mean since they finished the remodeling?" she asked, turning on the shower. "I checked it out after they left yesterday afternoon."

"No, I mean this morning. Did you come in here while I was in the shower?"

Rae shook her head. "No. Why?"

"Did anyone else come in here?" he asked.

"No. They aren't supposed to come in here, or the bedroom."

"I know," he said.

"Did you see someone?" she asked.

"No. I just had a strange feeling. Don't worry about it."

"Do you want me to check with..."

"No," he interrupted. "It was probably just me getting used to the new surroundings. Or maybe I was still dreaming in the shower."

"Well you better stop the day-dreaming or you're going to be late for work," she said, moving back toward him, tugging on the robe, flipping his hair and kissing his lips. "What kind of message would it send to be late for your first day on the job, Mr. President?"

CHAPTER 2

Wednesday, January 21, 2037
The White House

President Martin checked his wristwatch as he eased himself into his high-back leather chair behind the desk in the Oval Office. 5:59 a.m.

The marble desk clock also read 5:59, as did the wall clock across the room.

Presidential objective number one is a success, he thought.

"Good morning, Mr. President," came a voice from the main door. Gwen Hardin walked briskly toward the desk, dressed in a crisp beige business suit and carrying a notebook and several folders. She was as polished as the clock on the President's desk and every bit as punctual.

"Good morning Ms. Hardin," said the President. "Right on time, as always. No ill-effects from last night?"

"No, sir. Sound asleep by midnight."

"Midnight, how did you manage that? We were only on stop number five by midnight, with two more to go."

Gwen sat an open folder in front of the President. "That's the difference between being the President and being the President's secretary."

"Don't tell me you weren't invited to every inaugural ball on the planet," said the President, fingering the papers in the folder. "I know better than that."

"Oh, I was invited. But I had the luxury of turning most of them down. I just told everyone I had to get to work early today and train the new guy."

The quip brought a grin to the President's face. She may have been joking, but she was right. Gwen had been the single most important member of his transition team. She attached herself to the former President's secretary, less than a week after the election, and had worked tirelessly, right through the holidays.

Pushing 60, Gwen was razor-sharp and easily the most efficient executive assistant he had ever met. That's why he took her with him when he left the corporate world to embark on a political career many years ago. She had an eye for detail and a personal demeanor that fit every situation. Moreover, her judgment and perspective were always right on target. She would have held a prominent position on his campaign staff had she been more amenable to the rigorous travel schedule. Still, when Gwen called with congratulations on the day after he won the Independent Party nomination, he asked her to consider joining him in the White House "not if, but when" he won the election. She quickly agreed, noting that early retirement did not suit her well.

"Needless to say, you have an impossible schedule today," said Gwen, tapping the top page on the President's stack of papers. "At least you will be well-fed. There are three lunches and two dinners on the docket."

"Good," said the President. "I skipped breakfast. Where do we start?"

"Incoming and outgoing defense secretaries at 6:30. Mr. Kingman is scheduled for 7:30. There are several short meetings after that, but since they will likely get shuffled around, there is no use talking about them now. I will keep your PIB up-to-date."

The President fingered a dark grey ring on his right middle finger. A Personal Informatics and Biometrics device, commonly known as a PIB, had been around for more than a decade. They were now as common as cellphones and computer tablets had been at the turn of the century, but had since made both obsolete. While many still used the removable wrist or finger version, most executives now opted for the implanted ring which was surgically attached onto the right middle finger with a 10-minute outpatient procedure. The implanted version significantly increased both security and biometric functionality.

Removing or replacing the implant was considerably more painful, as Martin had learned two days earlier. Despite his initial objection, he was required to give up his personal PIB for an ultra-secure presidential PIB. His new PIB worked much like the old one, but with a few more bells and whistles.

Martin squeezed the ring between his left thumb and index finger and twisted slightly. A small holographic image of the presidential seal appeared above the ring. He raised his right hand to eye-level and looked directly into the seal as a thin beam of red light scanned his iris. The seal faded, replaced by several more transparent icons that floated just above the fingers on his right hand. He manipulated the icons by raising and lowering his fingers. It looked as if he was playing piano with one hand.

"Do you have that thing figured out yet?" asked Gwen.

"For the most part," he said, fingering through the icons and then tapping to bring up a holographic image of his schedule. "They still haven't told me which button launches the missiles."

Gwen nodded and gave the President a wry smile. She picked up the folders and papers and turned to leave. "Well, the guys with all the answers will be here in a few minutes. I'm sure they will cover it with you."

"Anything I can do for you, Ms. Hardin?" asked the President, as she neared the door.

"You could give me an exorbitant pay raise," answered Gwen, without stopping. Which was word-for-word the same answer that she had given Martin every time he had asked that question for the last two decades.

Martin tapped-off his PIB and leaned back in his chair. He surveyed the office, noting that all of the furniture had already been replaced. In keeping with tradition, the incoming President had redecorated the executive office. A couple weeks ago he had selected new drapes, sofas, chairs and tables which were all now in place. Just yesterday morning he had sat with the outgoing President on the outgoing chairs. The furniture had been replaced overnight, as had the drapes.

He had also selected a new paint scheme, more Earth tones than the current colors. He had requested that the painting be done several weeks later when he was scheduled to be away from the White House for a few days.

His attention returned to the desk, which was the most meaningful change. Since the late 1800s, most Presidents had used the same Resolute Desk in the Oval Office. The desk was a gift from Great Britain. It was named after the H.M.S. Resolute, a British ship which was abandoned in Artic ice while on a rescue mission in the 1850s. When the ice thawed, the ship drifted south into the Atlantic where it was discovered by a fishing boat and towed back to the States. The U.S. government had the ship refurbished and presented back to the British government as a gesture of friendship. After 20 more years of service, it was decommissioned. Queen Victoria had a desk made from it. She presented the desk to President Rutherford B. Hayes. The desk has been used by most Presidents since Hayes. Just a few Presidents had opted to use other desks, including Martin's grandfather, James Warren Patrick.

President Patrick had been life-long friends with a craftsman named Henry Arnall, who specialized in building office furniture. He had presented Patrick with a desk when he became Governor of Missouri. Patrick brought the desk to Washington, with the intent of using it in his office in the White House residence. But a few weeks into his administration, and without explanation, he had the desk moved to the Oval Office. The Resolute Desk was sent to the Smithsonian for temporary public display.

On the day that James Warren Patrick left office, the Resolute Desk was returned to the Oval Office where it had remained until last night.

Welcome back, thought Martin as he ran a palm across the polished desktop. He had sat at this desk a number of times as a small child, usually on his grandfather's lap. He had also spent a brief moment seated at the desk during the dedication of the James Warren Patrick Presidential Library when he was a teenager.

The Arnall family, now several generations older, but still producing magnificent furniture, had contacted Martin when he joined the Senate, offering to build him a desk. Martin politely declined, but agreed that if he ever made it to the White House he would accept the offer. His desk was now under construction in a small town in southwest Missouri, garnering much attention from the local media. The special walnut wood that was being used needed to cure for several days after each step in the construction process. The desk was on target for completion in late-February.

In the meantime, Martin had decided to use his grandfather's desk. He had little trouble convincing the library to allow the desk to return to the West Wing, especially since the library's curator was his sister.

His grandfather's time in office had predated the computer revolution. The desk that Martin remembered had always been cluttered with papers, file folders, and the fanciest phone he had ever seen. Whenever he had visited the Oval Office his grandfather would let him push a button on the phone, any button that he wanted, but only one. The phone had hundreds of buttons, many of them with lights. He remembered what a difficult time he had deciding which button to push.

Times had certainly changed. In the years following the Patrick administration, the Resolute Desk had been altered to accommodate several different phone systems and an ever-changing array of computer equipment. Large desktop boxes, with clunky monitors, gave way to floor towers with sleeker flat panel screens. Then there were the portable laptops with docking stations. The latest evolution was a flat sheet of glass that fit across the top of the desk and served as a work surface, a massive computer screen, keyboard, television and a fully integrated phone system. Many executives went through the workday without placing anything on their desk, except their hands and fingers.

Martin was disappointed to learn that his grandfather's desk would have had to be significantly altered to accommodate the glasstop technology. Since neither he, nor his sister, would have allowed that to happen, Martin opted for a portable glasstop phone system on the desktop. They installed a smaller glasstop computer system on the coffee table in the middle of the Oval Office. Otherwise, he would rely on his PIB, and in a pinch, a good old-fashioned piece of paper.

Martin tapped the Speaker icon on his glasstop phone. Within seconds, Gwen greeted him. "Yes, sir."

"Please give Deanna Faye at the Patrick Library a call this morning," said the President. "Tell her the desk arrived safe and sound, but that I was disappointed that there were not any chocolate-chip cookies stashed away in the drawers."

"Will do, Mr. President," said Gwen.

CHAPTER 3

Wednesday, January 21, 2037
The White House

At first glance, the two generals seated in the middle of the Oval Office were near identical. Both wore the standard blue Army service uniform. Both bore four mirror-finished silver stars on their shoulders. Countless ribbons and medals adorned both men's chest.

The outgoing Defense Secretary, Craig Bolser, was dark-complected with short-cropped silver hair, and a steady gaze that reflected almost three decades of military service. Bolser had spent the last half hour briefing the President on a myriad of national security concerns. This was standard practice during the transition of administrations. Partisan politics took a back seat to national security during times of transition or threat.

During this time, it was obvious that the incoming Defense Secretary, Wilbert Knudsen, had something else on his mind. He was participating in the discussions and adding appropriate comments. Yet there was something about him that did not sit right with the President. He was not as focused as usual. He was nervously picking at his fingernails and continually scratching at the back of his rust-red hair. What's more, he had glanced at the wall clock at least three times since the meeting began.

Up until now, Knudsen had been complementary of Bolser and his staff for the way they were handling themselves during the handover. Knudsen had been working with the previous administration's staff in an unofficial capacity until his official swearing-in yesterday afternoon.

President Martin had talked with Knudsen at the first inaugural ball early last evening. Everything seemed fine then. Knudsen was leaving for "one more meeting with Bolser" before making the social rounds later that night. Come to think of it, Martin had not seen him again all evening.

General Bolser was wrapping up the final agenda topic. It was apparent the security briefing was not going to take the full hour that had been allotted. Perhaps he would ask Knudsen to stay behind and give him a chance to talk more openly.

"Mr. President, there is one more topic that requires discussion that does not appear on the formal meeting agenda," said Bolser, reaching for his briefcase and punching a code into the keypad. Knudsen's pale eyebrows narrowed as he fixated on the briefcase. His face reddened, making his freckles more prominent.

"As you are aware," continued Bolser, "there are certain matters of national security that require the attention of only the highest levels of our government." He opened his briefcase revealing a second metallic cover and scanning screen. Bolser laid his left hand across the screen and leaned forward to allow his iris to be scanned. He then lifted the metallic cover and retrieved a large envelope and a pen-shaped device.

"With a couple of exceptions, what I am going to show you today is eyes-only," said Bolser, aiming the pen toward the President's PIB. "You may keep these documents."

Martin's PIB glowed and displayed an icon. After a couple of seconds, another page appeared. Knudsen activated his PIB and retrieved the same document.

"Secretary Knudsen received a similar briefing last night, with instructions to do nothing until after this meeting. From this moment forward, he will take directions on the matter directly from you and no one else."

Martin gave Bolser an affirming nod and looked at Knudsen.

"This is a list of every living person with direct and full knowledge of this matter," explained Bolser. "The date next to each name is the last time they were briefed."

Martin read through the list, estimating that there were a few dozen names, mostly former U.S. Presidents and high-ranking defense staff. The last name on the list was Wilbert M. Knudsen with yesterday's date.

Bolser referred the President to subsequent pages with several more names. "This list contains the names of all people, living or dead, who have, or had, full knowledge of this matter."

Again, Martin noted mostly senior defense staff and former Presidents, including his grandfather. The first name on the list was Harry S. Truman.

"This has been going for almost a century?" asked Martin, moving to the edge of his seat. "I'm intrigued to say the least."

"Are you familiar with the Roswell, New Mexico stories that were so popular at the end of the twentieth century?" asked Bolser.

"Sure," said the President. "Crashed UFOs, alien autopsies, Hollywood made a mint off of all that science-fiction hype."

"Indeed," said Bolser. "There was a great deal of hype. But not as much fiction as you might think." He pulled several photographs from the envelope and passed them to the President. Martin sorted through the pictures, laying them one-on-top-of-the-other on the table in front of them. They were black and white glossies of wreckage, victims and landscapes, followed by a series of surgical close-ups taken in a medical facility of some sort.

"These pictures have been in every documentary ever produced about Roswell," said the President. "I could pull them up on the Internet right now."

"That's true, Mr. President," said Bolser. "With a few exceptions, these photos have been in the public domain for many years. Some right after the incident."

"But you are telling me these are real?" said the President. "These are photos of an actual crash scene, with an actual spacecraft and actual alien bodies?"

"Yes, sir," said Bolser.

The President tossed the final few photos on the table and sat back in his chair. He let out an audible breath, as his face grew noticeably redder. "Secretary Bolser, is this some kind of hazing or practical joke? Like when Clinton stole all the Ws from the White House keyboards on his way out of office? I'm all for a good laugh, but my schedule…"

"Respectfully, sir," interrupted Knudsen. "This is not a joke. There's much more. And it's very real."

Martin locked eyes with Knudsen. The focus had returned.

Bolser pulled out the final item from the envelope, a dark grey metallic sheet roughly the size of a standard piece of paper. It was about an eighth of an inch thick and had a jagged tear across one side.

"Much of the additional evidence that you will want to review is housed at the Pentagon," said Bolser. "We can arrange for you to view the items at your discretion. This is a small sample."

Bolser held the sheet in both hands, and with some effort, began to crush and crinkle the item. He held the ball between his cupped hands a few inches above the table, then dropped it. The ball immediately began to unfold and unwrinkle. Within a few seconds, it had regained its original shape and lay unblemished, except for the jagged tear, in front of the President.

Martin carefully picked up the sheet. It was about the size of one of the photos, but weighed much less. In fact, the weight was imperceptible. Several symbols and markings had been etched into the sheet. They almost glowed from within, making the symbols and words appear as a hazy purple light on the dark grey page. He turned the sheet over to reveal more markings.

"Is this metal or paper?" asked the President, straining to repeat the same crushing procedure as Bolser; dropping the ball on the table with the same result.

"We don't know," answered Bolser. "We have been studying that material for almost ninety years and we still know nothing about it."

Martin again picked up the sheet and began to fold it end-to-end using the table top to crease each edge. After several folds, he laid the sheet on the table. The sheet immediately began to unfold itself, again appearing perfectly smooth except for the jagged edge.

"And the tear?" said Martin.

Bolser picked up the sheet. "It appears there is a four-to-five inch section of the sheet missing. It was never found." He pulled hard on the tear. "We have tried everything from diamond blades to lasers to continue that tear. Nothing."

"How much of this stuff exists?" asked Martin.

"Quite a bit," answered Bolser. "It appears that both the interior and exterior of the craft was made from the same material. We have several very large pieces and many pieces this size and smaller. All of it is housed at the Pentagon."

"Have we put any of it back together?" asked Knudsen. Apparently, the conversation had gone down a different trail than the one he heard the night before.

"We've identified which pieces should fit together, but we have not found a way to reattach them," said Bolser, handing the piece back to the President. "It does not respond to welding or riveting. While we've never been able to separate a piece, or alter its form, we can't find a way to put it back together, other than with a computer simulation."

Turning his attention back to the symbols, the President moved the sheet to-and-fro in front of his eyes, like someone trying to get used to new bifocals. Not only did the symbols come in and out of focus, they appeared to move around on the page, and in some cases, change completely.

"What about the markings?" asked Martin. "Has anyone been able to get them to hold still long enough to decipher them?"

"We have made some progress in that area," answered Bolser. "There are some people at the Pentagon who can explain that better than I."

"I have some briefings scheduled at the Pentagon early next week," said the President, handing the sheet back to Bolser. "Let's make sure we add this to the docket."

"Actually, Mr. President, you may want to fast-track this," said Bolser, returning the sheet and photos to the envelope and repacking his briefcase. "What we have been able to learn, thus far, suggests that we could be in imminent danger." Bolser paused briefly to let his words sink in. "The general belief is that this craft was on a mission to deliver a message."

Knudsen and the President exchanged glances, both sensing a change in Bolser's tone of voice. "Go on," said the President.

"Several sheets such as this one, along with other pieces of equipment found within the craft, have led us to believe that this craft was one of many," said Bolser. "Further, we believe those craft were intent on returning, in the future, with the goal of habitation."

"Habitation?" said the President. "As in, invasion?"

"Yes, sir," answered Bolser. "There were a number of materials that clearly show these beings had a thorough understanding of the Earth's geography and atmosphere. It's evident that they had long term plans for extensive habitation."

"You can tell all of that from symbols like the ones you just showed me?" asked Martin.

"Yes," said Bolser. "Symbols like these and other pieces of equipment. It can be better explained at the Pentagon facilities."

Martin leaned back in his chair and ran a hand through his hair. He understood that Bolser's objective in this meeting was to get his attention, which he most certainly had done.

"I don't suppose we have been able to come up with a timeline for this habitation?" asked the President.

"Actually, sir, we have," said Bolser. "August."

"August?" repeated Martin.

"August of this year, Mr. President," said Bolser.

"Let me guess," said Martin. "I'll need to go to the Pentagon to better understand how we came up with August of this year?"

"That would be best, sir," answered Bolser.

Martin stood and walked toward the glass door leading to the Rose Garden. After a moment of looking outside, he tapped his PIB and fingered to the "GH" icon. "Ms. Hardin. Please find a couple of hours for a trip to the Pentagon this afternoon. Move whatever you need to move. This is priority. Coordinate with Secretary Knudsen and General Bolser."

Knudsen and Bolser stood and walked with the President toward the main Oval Office door.

"Secretary Knudsen," said the President. "I need you to learn as much as you can, as fast as you can, from General Bolser and his staff. Start building a list of people you need to bring onboard, but talk with me before briefing anyone else." The President turned to Bolser. "Obviously I'm going to need some help with this. I think your list is going to grow."

"That is your call, Mr. President," said Bolser. "I'll play whatever role you wish. I'll see you this afternoon."

CHAPTER 4

Wednesday, January 21, 2037
The White House

President Martin sat at his desk flipping through virtual pages from his PIB. His departure for the Pentagon was scheduled for 2 p.m. He would have a solid hour and a half before he needed to return to the White House.

He had barely dipped into his morning schedule and was already faced with a national emergency, or rather a planetary emergency of epic proportion. Martin prided himself on being a problem-solver. That characteristic had propelled him into a corner office with a major telecommunications firm early in his career.

Planetary invasion by an advanced race of aliens of whom we know nothing about, he thought. *I wonder if that would be classified as a merger or an acquisition.*

A slight click from the phone speaker on his glasstop interrupted his thought.

"Mr. Kingman is here," said Gwen.

"Send him in," replied the President, standing and walking around the desk.

The door leading to Gwen's office opened. A tall, fit, well-dressed, middle-aged man entered. Y. Alan Kingman was the savviest person Martin had ever met. They had been best friends since college. Kingman had immediately jumped into the Washington political mix after graduation, while Martin headed for the corporate world. They had stayed in touch, mostly through Kingman's continued ranting about how Martin needed to "do something real with his life." Kingman served as an outside consultant when Martin decided to run for Governor in his home state of Missouri. When Martin decided to make the leap to the U.S. Senate, Kingman piloted the campaign.

Kingman was book smart and had spent enough time in Washington to know how things got done. He hated the political process but could play the game with the best of them. He had run Martin's staff in the Senate, managed his presidential campaign, and was the only name on the list when Martin selected a Chief of Staff.

The only thing Kingman hated more than political rhetoric was his first name. Martin had made the mistake of using it in public one time back in their early college days. Kingman turned beet red and stayed that way for close to a week. At six-foot-six-inches tall, Kingman was more than half a foot taller than Martin and easily outweighed him by 60 pounds. As a means of self-preservation, Martin had since opted to use Kingman's last name, or his preferred nickname, Yak.

The President met his Chief of Staff in the middle of the room and firmly shook his hand. "Good morning, Yancy. Welcome to the Oval Office."

"You did NOT just call me that," said Kingman, gripping the President's hand tighter. The red from his neck was moving north.

"I just think since we now occupy two of the most powerful positions in the country, we should use our given names," said the President, trying miserably to match Yak's tight grasp.

Kingman kept the grip and leaned down toward the President's ear. "What makes you think I won't slam you down on the floor and pound the life out of you?"

"I'm counting on the dozen or so Secret Service guys who would be in here in a second if you tried that."

"I could take 'em," said Kingman, releasing the President's hand. The red was fading.

"How about you let this one slide if I agree to never use that name again?" asked Martin.

"What's in it for me?"

"You get to keep this glamorous new job," replied Martin. "And you get to help me figure out what to do with this blazing hot potato I just got handed."

"Potatoes already?" asked Kingman. "They don't waste any time."

"Just your basic everyday alien invasion," said the President.

"What, the coast-to-coast fences they built in the 2020s aren't holding?" asked Kingman.

"Different kind of alien," replied Martin. "We would need a much higher fence to keep these out."

Ten minutes later, the men were sitting on opposite ends of the sofa. President Martin had recounted the discussion he had with Bolser and Knudsen earlier that morning. So far, Kingman had not said a word. But, based on his wide-eyed expression, he had a firm grasp of the magnitude of the situation.

Gwen entered from her office and waited for the President to acknowledge her with a glace. "President Rosemont is calling. Is this a good time?"

The President pointed toward the glasstop unit on the coffee table in front of the sofa. "I'll take it here in a moment. Thanks Gwen."

Kingman started to rise to allow the President to take the call in private.

"Stay," said the President. "I'm pretty sure you already know what this call is about." He tapped the flashing icon.

"Good Morning, Mr. President," said Martin. "How's the first day of retirement treating you?"

"I imagine I'm a bit less busy than you," said Rosemont. "They have installed a secure line in my home office. We can speak freely."

"Alan Kingman is here with me," said Martin. "I have been briefing him on my meeting with Secretary Bolser this morning."

"You have no idea how sorry I am to hit you with that right out of the gate, James," said Rosemont. "I know that's not what you signed-up for."

"I assumed you would leave me some unfinished business, but isn't this a little extreme?" said Martin.

"Believe me, had I found a viable solution, I would have acted immediately," said Rosemont. "I spent the first three years in office thinking the brains at NASA would come up with something. You need to get to the Pentagon to see what they have for yourself."

"That's set for this afternoon," said Martin, quickly hitting the mute icon and pointing to Kingman. "I want you with me for that meeting."

Kingman nodded as Martin pressed the mute again.

"I noticed you didn't involve many of your staff on this issue," said Martin.

"True," said Rosemont. "I wanted to uncover some possible solutions first, but they never came. Next thing I knew I was left with no option, but to keep quiet and pass the buck, just like everyone before me."

"How ironic is that?" asked Martin. "This whole thing started with Truman. I thought he was a buck-stopper, not a buck-starter."

"I've had that thought," said Rosemont. "When you decide what you're going to do with this century-old buck, please let me know. I suspect I will be even more popular then."

"I will keep you in the loop, sir," said Martin. "Thanks for the call."

Martin disconnected, sat back on the sofa, and blew out a breath. "Pretty much what I expected."

Kingman shrugged. "It fits his track record."

Joseph J. Rosemont had endured the most unpopular presidency of the 21st century. Plagued by countless domestic and foreign challenges, Rosemont had become infamous for his inaction. During his four-year administration, the economy had spiraled out of control, the deficit ballooned, and the American public had lost confidence in government to a point not seen since the early 2000s.

Just before the beginning of his fourth year in office, Rosemont surpassed lame-duck status and became a sitting-duck when the GOP made it clear that the incumbent would not receive his party's nomination. The Republican powerbase then took turns tripping over each other, positioning themselves to take Rosemont's place. By the time the primaries were over, it was a two-man race between Martin and the Democratic candidate.

This was when Kingman took over. He wrapped Martin in the legacy left by his grandfather and topped him with the crown jewels of the nation's youngest and fastest growing political party.

The Independent Action Party (IAP) had achieved political prominence by winning three straight presidential elections. They recast the image of the American presidency, promoting action-oriented corporate leaders including the nation's first female President. Moreover, the IAP molded public expectation. Partisan bickering and career speechmakers were out. Action was in.

Martin had proven his ability to promote change and action in the corporate world, as well as during his two terms as Missouri's Governor. He rode that resume to the Senate. While most Senators preferred to slip in and out the back door, Martin asked to be seated in the front of the chamber. This quickly established him as a force to be dealt with among the Washington elite. Soon his IAP cohorts followed suit, resulting in another change to the political status quo. Now, it was Democrats to the left of the aisle, Republicans to the right of the aisle, and Independents in the front.

James Patrick Martin was the action candidate in a time that Americans desperately needed action. He won the election in a landslide.

That was three months ago. Now, less than a day into their new positions, President Martin and his top advisor were rearranging their agendas. They had been handed a new priority.

CHAPTER 5

Wednesday, January 21, 2037
Washington, D.C.

Rudolph Overton had always known how he would die. As that
time drew nearer, he became more and more obsessed by the
thought.

He stood at the window, sipping from a ceramic mug and staring at the Washington Monument, which was just visible through
the morning mist on the distant horizon.

"Would you like some more tea, sir?" asked a voice from the
doorway.

"No, thank you," said Overton, shifting his gaze upward. The
morning fog was beginning to lift. It would be a clear day across the
city.

He turned from the window and made his way across the study
to a large desk. He was still wearing a silk dressing robe, which was
unusual for this time of the morning, but he'd had a late night.

Another inauguration, how many has it been now? Ten? Maybe
twelve? He reached for the embossed invitation on the corner of the
desk, then opened a drawer and retrieved a hanging file. He placed
the invitation on top of the stack. He hoped that, perhaps, this would
be the last one.

He lowered his rangy frame into the chair and surveyed the top
of the desk. His work area was always free of clutter, and often
completely bare, aside from a phone and a worn wooden box that
was ever-present in the middle of the desk. As he did most every
morning, Overton pulled the box closer and fished a long silver
chain from under his shirt collar. Leaning forward, the chain was
just long enough to allow him to slip the attached key into the lock

on the front of the box. He hesitated a few seconds before opening the lid, his eyes wide with anticipation, like a child opening a surprise gift. But this was no surprise. Overton was very familiar with the contents of the box. They had been with him his entire life, throughout his long journey. They were the three most precious items in the world.

As he peered into the box, subdued chimes began from an ornate grandfather clock that dominated the other side of the room.

Eight o'clock, he thought. *By now President Martin would have been briefed. Now he knows.*

CHAPTER 6

Wednesday, January 21, 2037
Washington, D.C.

Even at idle speed, the rotor blades of the Marine One helicopter created a powerful wind rush and deafening noise. Martin and Kingman had just climbed the short steps into the cabin and were strapped into their seats. The craft rose above the south lawn and turned southwest for the four-minute flight to the Pentagon.

The third passenger in the aircraft was Chris Boone. As head of the Secret Service detail assigned to the White House, Agent Boone was ultimately in charge of the President's personal security. He traveled with Martin whenever he left the White House, be that for a trip around the globe or a trip across the city. Boone was short in stature, but built like an NFL linebacker. His crew cut and trimmed goatee made him look menacing when straight-faced and like a teddy bear when he smiled. This explained why he rarely smiled.

Since this afternoon's destination was the Pentagon, Boone was the only White House agent assigned to the trip. They would rely on Secret Service agents stationed at the Pentagon, as well as the Pentagon's massive security force, for the required protection.

The noise was muted inside the cabin, but still too loud for conversation without the aid of headphones.

Kingman motioned out the window, toward a large skyboard that was replaying President Martin's inaugural address. Martin glanced at the enormous image and shook his head slowly. He still could not get used to seeing himself hovering overhead like something out of a science-fiction film.

NASA had perfected this technology about a decade ago. Media satellites orbiting the earth could project video images in the sky a few hundred feet above the ground. Anyone within a 10-mile radius had a perfectly clear view of the image, regardless of their viewing angle. Audio waves were also emitted from the satellites and automatically adjusted, based on distance from the image, so that the audio was in perfect time with the video.

In the beginning, an expensive ground-based receiver was required to link-up with the satellite. This limited the technology to large urban areas. Over the last few years, the techno-wizardry had advanced to the point that the ground receiver was no longer needed. The PIB devices that most people wore picked up the audio signals and translated them into the user's preferred language. This meant images and sound could be projected anywhere on Earth.

Kingman and Boone continued to survey the Washington landscape while the President checked his watch: 2:01 p.m. A vision of the coin from the bathroom that morning flashed in his mind.

Martin tapped his PIB, accessing his calendar and fingering to the page marked "Original." He had originally been scheduled for "Open Time" from 2:00 to 2:10 p.m.

Martin again thought about how that coin seemed to just appear out of nowhere on the bathroom vanity. Oddly, it was no longer the strangest moment of the day.

He had a feeling that trend would continue.

CHAPTER 7

Wednesday, January 21, 2037
The Pentagon

General Craig Bolser greeted the President and Chief of Staff as they exited the helicopter. The engines and rotors had been shut off and were winding down, providing a welcome respite from the pounding noise.

The group walked quickly into the building, past several security personnel, to a waiting elevator. Agent Boone positioned himself outside the elevator, seamlessly turning over responsibility for the President's protection to the Pentagon staff. An Air Force Sergeant saluted as the remaining men entered and then pressed a series of numbers into a keypad. The doors shut and the elevator began a rapid decent.

"We are going to the lowest level of the building," said Bolser. "This area was built in 1947, just two years after the primary construction project was over. This level is known as Majestic. Everyone with access to this level has top-secret clearance."

"How deep are we?" asked the President.

"About three stories below ground level," answered Bolser. The elevator slowed to a stop.

"So much for five rings, five levels, five layers," said the President.

Bolser just grinned.

The doors opened to reveal a long hallway. Four soldiers stood at attention, two on each side of the hall. They saluted in unison as the men passed. A fifth guard stood inside an open doorway flanked by Wilbert Knudsen.

Knudsen shook hands with Kingman and nodded toward the President. "Mr. President. Mr. Kingman."

"Good to see you again, General," said Kingman.

"Did you get this all figured out?" asked Martin.

Knudsen sighed. "Hardly, sir. But I do have a better picture of what we are dealing with."

"Lead the way," said Martin.

Bolser and Knudsen escorted the group past several more guards into a warehouse-like room about the size of an airline hangar. The walls were made up of several standard size garage doors. Two larger doors were on the far wall in front of them. The men descended a flight of stairs and proceeded along a metal walkway leading to a raised platform in the middle of the room. Three technicians, who had been seated at computer consoles, stood as the group reached the platform. A woman stood in the middle of the platform. Like the technicians, she wore a white lab coat.

"This is our Chief Engineer from NASA, Dr. Emily Lindsey," said Bolser. "She runs the show here."

"Welcome, Mr. President, Mr. Kingman," said Lindsey, peering over a pair of reading glasses. "Shall we get started?"

"Please," said Martin.

Lindsey turned as the technicians returned to their seats and started typing on virtual keypads. Each of the doors on the walls in the room began to rise, and platforms extended from within the walls toward the center of the room. Each platform held a number of dark grey metal segments of various sizes. Two of the pieces were the size of large automobiles, ranging downward to the size of a beach ball.

"These are the largest items that were recovered from the crash site," said Lindsey. "The smaller items are stored in an adjoining room. In total, there are 114 pieces. Based on our computer modeling, we believe that every piece that made up the physical structure of the craft was recovered. This includes 103 of the segments. The other 11 pieces are believed to be free standing materials from within the craft. All of the internal pieces are intact. However some–like the item you saw this morning–are damaged to some degree."

Lindsey glanced at one of the technicians who punched several buttons on her keyboard. The platform from the far wall, which held the two largest pieces, moved closer to the viewing platform. A large video screen descended from the ceiling and hung directly above the pieces.

"The most telling pieces are the largest and smallest," said Lindsey. "We'll show you the small pieces later."

She raised a device that looked like a small flashlight and pointed it toward one of the large segments. A section of the piece glowed with a pale blue light. The video screen displayed a magnified image of the section targeted by Lindsey. Everyone on the viewing platform alternated glances between the piece on the platform and the video screen.

"These pieces are our best examples of the external and internal sections of the craft that remained intact," said Lindsey, aiming the blue light deep inside the structure. "This section was part of the propulsion system."

The video screen displayed an array of integrated components that seamlessly fit together to form a single solid mass of grey metal. The piece vaguely resembled a combustion engine, but without bolts or seams.

"It looks like everything is made from the same material," said the President.

"That's an accurate assessment," said Lindsey. "We haven't found anything connected to the craft that is made from anything other than the flexible grey material. No wires, no lubricants, nothing that we would consider a fuel source." She focused on another large piece. "This section is the bottom of the craft. We assume this held more of the propulsion system, including the fuel source. But we aren't sure. We have found no way to break through the material and it does not respond to x-ray, laser scanning, or resonance imaging."

The President shook his head in amazement. "So we really don't have any idea what type of metal this is?"

"Actually, sir," said Lindsey. "We can't even classify this as metallic. Nothing we have found appears anywhere on our Periodic Chart. It behaves unlike any metal we've seen. Some pieces are very flexible; you can bend them by hand. Others are so rigid that we have not been able to alter them at all."

Lindsey turned and whispered something to one of the technicians. The young lady nodded, rose from her seat, and walked down a set of stairs in front of the viewing stand. She stepped onto the platform and stood directly in front of one of the largest segments. The top of the piece extended a couple of feet over her head.

"Natalie is going to demonstrate the most unusual characteristic of the material," said Lindsey.

Natalie turned, bent down, and gripped the bottom of the piece, then effortlessly raised the entire segment over her head. She then turned her body, and the piece, to face the group.

"My God!" said Kingman. "She's not even straining."

Natalie shifted her balance and lowered one arm. She then began to toss the piece up and down several inches in the air. After a few seconds, she returned the piece to the platform and climbed the stairs back to the viewing stand.

Kingman's eyes followed Natalie all the way back to her seat. "Even if that were made out of balloons and Styrofoam, she should not have been able to do that. How much does that weigh?"

"It doesn't," said Lindsey. "At least, not that we've been able to measure. And we've used the most sensitive scales available."

The President moved toward the railing of the viewing stand to get a closer look at the piece. "A weightless aircraft?"

"Yes, sir," said Lindsey. "General Knudsen was asking how that would affect flight dynamics last night."

Knudsen nodded and continued Lindsey's thought. "You have to wonder how this would react to things like wind shear and g-forces."

"We've placed all of these pieces in wind tunnels, several times," explained Lindsey. "They don't move at all. The laws of physics, as we understand them, do not apply."

Lindsey turned again and said something to one of the technicians. After a flurry of key strokes, the platforms holding the large pieces retracted toward the walls, creating a void in the center of the room next to the viewing stand. The video screen ascended back into the ceiling and was replaced by an oblong device with several glass lenses. After a few seconds, the device began to hum. Faint lights appeared behind the lenses, much like a data projector. Kingman joined the President along the railing and noticed a similar device rising from beneath an opening in the floor.

"I mentioned our computer modeling earlier, Mr. President," said Lindsey, motioning toward the void between the projectors in the center of the room. "This will give you a better perspective of what the craft looked like in its original state."

A holographic image of a semi-circular structure appeared as if it were hovering in the air. It was the width of a large fighter jet, yet taller in the mid-section. The edges of the outer portion of the craft were rounded, and the bottom of the craft was flatter than the top. Lindsey used another flashlight-shaped device to control the holograph. The image rotated slightly and tilted upward, exposing the top of the craft to the viewing stand. From this angle, it was the shape of a third-quarter moon, perfectly round on the front and sides, but missing the back section, as if another craft had taken a bite out of it.

"The 103 larger pieces stored in this room fit together perfectly to form this image," said Lindsey, slowly rotating the craft and alternating the slant to show the top and bottom of the image. "All of the edges are rounded. In fact, there is no flat surface anywhere on the outside of the craft."

As the front of the craft rotated to a stop facing the viewing stand, Lindsey aimed the blue light at the top tier of the craft. That section of the holograph changed color, and one of the platforms from along the wall moved toward the center of the room. The piece on the platform corresponding to the highlighted section of the hologram was bathed in light from the ceiling.

"This is the third largest piece that was recovered," said Lindsey. "We believe it represents an observation station or cockpit." She clicked more buttons and the highlighted section of the image disappeared revealing the interior of the craft. Other platforms extended from the walls toward the image and several individual pieces were illuminated from above. "As you can see, there is room for three Hecatians."

President Martin raised a hand. "Hecatians?"

"Yes, sir," said Lindsey, glancing at General Bolser. "That's what we call the aliens."

General Bolser stepped forward. "Mr. President, this is one of those things that makes much more sense with the help of Dr. Lindsey's visual aids."

Dr. Lindsey aimed her control device at a side section of the craft. "This symbol appears on the exterior of the craft in several places, much like the American flag and the NASA logo that appear on our spacecraft."

A glowing purple symbol appeared on the screen. It was a circle that enclosed a curving maze with three matching sections. A spiraling flame appeared in the center of the symbol.

"This symbol closely resembles an ancient Greek symbol known as a strophalos. One of the best-known is the Strophalos of Hecate. Hecate is an ancient Greek goddess believed to be associated with crossroads and entrance-ways to other worlds."

"Well that certainly seems appropriate," said the President.

Lindsey continued to highlight different sections of the craft as Knudsen and Kingman listened intently. Martin and Bolser walked back down the metal walkway toward the stairs.

"How big is the Majestic team?" asked Martin.

"There are eight on the scientific team. This is Lindsey's full team. You will meet the other group later," said Bolser. "Lindsey's group is focused on the craft. In the past, there have been as many as 10 on this group. Some of the previous team members are brought back to consult from time to time, usually when something new is discovered."

"How often do we discover something new?" asked Martin.

"It's been a long time," said Bolser. "The holographic imagery technology was enhanced a few years ago. Other than that, this is what we've worked with for the past two decades. We bring in new blood every few years, in the hope of coming up with new ideas. Dr. Lindsey has been on the team for the past 25 years. She was the one who came up with the original computer simulations that produced the image of the craft."

The President turned back toward the viewing stand. Knudsen and Kingman were now focused on different sections of the craft. Lindsey was still talking to Kingman. Two of the technicians were gathered around Knudsen.

"Where do we get the technicians?"

"Those three all graduated top of their classes with PhDs from MIT," answered Bolser.

"So that was three times our collective IQ Doctor Natalie hoisting the Buick over her head a few minutes ago?" said Martin.

Bolser smiled. "And then some. We hand-pick them as they are nearing graduation. We wipe out their student loans in exchange for them serving their country for a few years."

"How are they trained?" asked Martin.

"They spend about six months in technical orientation and project briefings," explained Bolser. "It takes about that long for the security clearance to be issued. Even after all of that, they are pretty surprised when they first see this room. It's not exactly what they signed up for."

President Martin shrugged. "I know the feeling."

CHAPTER 8

Wednesday, January 21, 2037
The Pentagon

Knudsen, Kingman and Lindsey joined the President and Bolser at the top of the stairs near the entrance to the warehouse room.

"I believe you will be meeting with my colleague, Dr. Gordon, next," said Lindsey. "I appreciate the opportunity to have met with you, Mr. President."

"This was very helpful Dr. Lindsey," said Martin, shaking her hand. "Please thank your team for us."

Bolser led the group down the hallway toward another door and another guard.

"The room we were just in is located below the A and B rings above," said Bolser. "This room is located directly below the outermost section of B ring." He nodded as the guard opened the door.

The group gathered near a large conference table at the front of the room. The room was the size of a large classroom and had the feel of a laboratory; tile floors, bright lights, lots of tables, computers and instruments. Along the longest wall was a row of waist-high display tables. Each held an item incased in a glass box.

"This room has some interesting history," said Bolser. "When the 747 crashed into the Pentagon during the 9/11 attack, earlier this century, the tip of the plane penetrated all the way into B ring, and deep into the sub-levels, stopping right above this room. The ensuing fire burned and smoldered for days. No one was in this room at the time of the crash. The entire level was evacuated without injury. Days later, when crews reached this room, everything in it was burnt and melted beyond recognition, except for these 11 pieces. They were strewn about the room, but completely undamaged."

The group moved closer to the row of display cases. Kingman ran a hand across one the of stainless steel tables. "It must have been like a smelting furnace in here."

"The temperature would have exceeded 1,500 degrees Fahrenheit," said Bolser.

President Martin was leaning over one of the display cases. "I assume these pieces are also weightless?"

"Yes," said Bolser.

"Weightless, yet indestructible," said Kingman, shaking his head in wonder. "This is some seriously advanced technology."

A middle-aged man entered the room from a side door and joined the group.

"This is Dr. Dennis Gordon," said Bolser. "He heads the research team that works with items from inside the craft."

Gordon acknowledged the introduction with a nod. "Good afternoon, Mr. President, gentlemen. Welcome to Majestic. I trust Dr. Lindsey's presentation was enlightening?"

"You have a hard act to follow, Dr. Gordon," said Martin.

"Let's get started," said Gordon, motioning toward a trio of technicians who had slipped in at the back of the room. The lights in the room dimmed, and the glass display cases glowed with internal light.

The first five cases each held a dark grey sheet, including the one with a jagged tear that Bolser had brought to the Oval Office that morning. They were all the same size and all contained similar symbols and markings, including the prominent strophalos.

In the remaining cases were six matching pieces, each about the size of a soda can. They were shaped like a bullet, with one end flattened, and the other ending in a rounded point. Protruding from one side of the device was a tab about the size of a tube of lipstick. It was attached near the flat end of the device and extended toward the pointed end. On the opposite side from the tab was a half-inch slit running the length of the device. The entire piece appeared to be made from the same dark grey metallic substance as the rest of the craft.

Gordon removed one of the bullet-shaped pieces from the display case as the group gathered around. "This is a respirator."

Everyone stared at the piece, too stunned to say anything.

"This part of the device attached to the user," said Gordon, turning the pointed end toward the floor and running his finger along the tab. "Waste product was emitted from this slit."

"What do you mean by *waste product*?" asked the President.

"If this were a human respirator, you would place this tab in your mouth," said Gordon. "Oxygen would flow through the tab as you breathed in, carbon dioxide would be pushed through the slit as you breathed out."

Kingman shifted his stance. "You're not saying this thing produces oxygen are you?"

"No," replied Gordon. "We don't know what it produces."

"How does it work?" asked Martin.

"We don't know," answered Gordon. "As with all of the materials, we've not been able to get inside."

"What about the slit?" asked Kingman.

Gordon took a penlight from his pocket and aimed the light inside the opening. "The slit is about an inch deep, and all we can see inside is more metal. The only difference between the inside metal and everything else we have seen is the color. The inside metal is black."

"If we can't see inside, and we don't have any idea how it works, we can only assume that it is a breathing device, right?" said the President.

"No, sir," said Gordon. "We are certain this is a type of respirator."

"How can you possibly be certain of something like that?" said Martin.

Gordon returned the device to the display case and nodded to the technicians. "Let me show you. Would you gentlemen please move toward the end of the room?"

A technician watched as the men shuffled toward the far wall. He then pressed a series of buttons on a control panel. A muted humming noise rose from beneath the center of the room as the floor split. Three metal tables ascended each holding bodies that could have been mistaken for human, if not for the inhuman shaped heads and the previous events of the day. Each body was enclosed in a glass cover.

Kingman took a small step forward, leaned downed and peered through the glass. "More models?" he asked. "Like the craft we saw earlier?"

All of men moved closer to the cases. Gordon inserted his arms into two access ports on the side of one of the glass cases. The attached gloves allowed him to manipulate the body without coming in direct contact with it. "No, sir," he said, raising one of the arms and bending it at the elbow. "These are the real deal. They were recovered from the crash site in New Mexico in 1945."

"Wouldn't they have decomposed by now?" asked the President. "They look unblemished."

"That's another of the many mysteries," said Gordon. "We don't know how, but we believe the outer covering of these bodies is actually a full body suit. Evidently the suit prevents decomposition."

Gordon motioned toward a port on the case closest to the President. "Feel the texture."

Martin tentatively inserted his arms into the port gloves and touched the arm of one of the bodies. He lifted the forearm slightly, noting it was flexible, almost lifelike. Then he ran his hand across the chest. It was pliable, like human skin, but had a mesh-like texture. The color was very unusual, not quite black, but not quite grey either. Martin stepped back and moved to the top of the table, reinserting his arms into a port closer to the head. He tried to pinch and lift the suit from the creature's neck, but the covering more closely resembled skin than clothing. He gazed deeply into the large orb-shaped eyes. The smooth black surface looked like an inky fluid. President Martin recoiled and let out a slight gasp when he saw his reflection in the eyes.

The eyes were mesmerizing, but the other facial features were nondescript, perhaps from being covered. The ears and nose were very small. Instead of protruding from the skull, they were slightly recessed, curving into the head. If orifices were present, they were not visible because of the covering. Above the pointed chin, and also under the covering, were the faint lines of a small mouth.

Stepping back from the body, Martin pointed toward the table holding a body that was lying face down. Kingman had already positioned himself at the head of the case and was running his hands across the back of the head.

"Are they all three the same?" asked Martin.

"As far as we can tell they are identical," said Gordon. "They are exactly the same height and weight. Visibly there are no differences."

"What is this hole in the back of the neck?" asked Kingman.

"Let me show you," said Gordon, nodding toward the video screen on the wall. "This will help answer your questions about the respirator."

The screen came to life. The familiar *U.S. Government Confidential* warnings were displayed, followed by a grey image of an operating room. Two exam tables were situated under large surgical lights. Each table held one body, one face up, one face down.

"This is one of the films from the original exams that were conducted in New Mexico during the first few weeks after the crash and retrieval," said Gordon. "The films previous to this one are uneventful, mostly frustrated personnel trying in vain to remove the outer coverings."

Three people, all wearing surgical scrubs and masks, came into frame on the video screen. A fourth person was behind the camera, adjusting the view.

"These are four members of the original medical team," explained Gordon. "The two men are physicians. The female is a nurse. The female behind the camera is also a nurse. We just have video, no sound."

The camera panned away from the exam tables and focused on a large plate glass viewing window. Through the glare in the window, three men in dark suits could be seen. The man closest to the window held a fedora in his hand.

President Martin moved closer to the video screen, intently studying the man behind the window. "I'll be damned. Is that Truman?"

General Bolser cleared his throat. "Yes, sir. That is indeed President Truman."

As Bolser spoke, Truman looked directly at the camera, frowned and motioned toward the exam tables. The camera was refocused on the body lying face down.

Kingman let out a short laugh. "Seems like he wasn't too pleased with having his presence documented."

The physicians positioned themselves each on one side of the body. The nurse was at the head of the table holding one of the respirator devices that Gordon had shown the group earlier.

Gordon took a remote from a side table and paused the video. "I should warn you that what you are about to see is quite disturbing."

President Martin nodded. "Go ahead."

The video resumed. As one of the physicians took the device from the nurse, the camera tightened focus on the back of the head. The physician slipped the tab of the device into the opening on the back of the neck. Both physicians and the nurse immediately took a step back from the table. After a few seconds, one physician laid his hand across the device and nodded emphatically. The nurse at the head of the table covered her face and began to convulse. When she lowered her hands, trails of black blood streamed from her eyes. She tried to retreat behind one of the physicians, but was blocked by his body, which was doubled-over in violent seizures. As the nurse and physician both tumbled to the floor, the second physician fell forward onto the exam table. He ripped the bloody mask from his face revealing inky blackness streaming from his eyes, nose and mouth. His body jerked upward a final time knocking the device from the body and onto the floor.

The image jerked as the nurse behind the camera stumbled forward. For a split second, her hand could be seen grasping toward the lens. She knocked the camera sideways, bringing the viewing window back into frame. President Truman could be seen, mouth agape, eyes wide and frozen in fear. The two men behind the President grabbed him by the shoulders, turned and moved quickly out of frame.

Again the image jerked, this time the camera fell forward landing directly in front of its operator. Silver-framed cat-eye spectacles, with spider-web cracks in each lens, slid from her face to the linoleum floor. She squinted slightly, and then peered deeply into the camera. A stream of oily blood dripped from her nose and mouth, pooling around the glasses, inching closer to the camera as the video continued to play.

CHAPTER 9

Wednesday, January 21, 2037
The White House

Rae Martin stepped into the residence portion of the White House a little after 9 p.m., after a long day of meetings, speeches and social gatherings. Her feet hurt and she was starving. She wondered how she could be hungry since every appointment on her calendar included some form of meal or refreshment. Come to think of it, she had never seen any of the food.

As she walked into the living room, her husband tapped his PIB to disconnect a phone call. She headed straight for the half-eaten BLT on the coffee table.

"Still running the country this late?" she asked, kissing him lightly on the lips before taking big bite of the sandwich.

"Actually, I was talking to the other woman in my life," James answered.

Rae chewed for a moment then swallowed. "How is mom today?"

"Stubborn as ever. I was trying one last time to strong-arm her into moving. She is apparently immune from my new-found executive powers."

James' mother, Betty Patrick Martin, was a saint of a woman who had spent most of the last decade caring for her husband, Joe. Betty and Joe were both in their mid-70s. Joe had been diagnosed with Alzheimer's shortly after he retired at age 65. At first the disease progressed slowly, with Joe showing few symptoms other than memory loss. But over the last few years he had grown more and more sullen, spending most of his day in bed, or in his recliner, staring at reruns of *I Love Lucy* or *M.A.S.H.* He still knew his wife, but rarely recognized anyone else. He understood that his son had won the presidency, but his only comment when Betty mentioned James Patrick was, "Proud of the pup."

For years, James had tried to coax his mother into moving to an assisted living center in D.C. For years, his mother had given him the same answer, "A move would be very difficult for your dad. We're fine right here."

The "right here" that she was so fond of was a beautiful house they had built 50 years ago, in Joplin, MO. It stood just a few miles from her childhood home, and just a few blocks from the Patrick Library. His parents had always been independent and self-sustaining. Betty was a high school teacher. Joe wrote biographies, including several volumes on his father-in-law. Betty was proud of her father and her lineage, but she was most happy in her house, away from the tourists and the press. She had reluctantly agreed to have a Secret Service detail stationed at the house after James won the election, but moving was absolutely out of the question.

James left home for the first time when he was a sophomore in high school to attend a prep school in the mountains surrounding Asheville, N.C. He returned to Joplin in the summers and lived with his parents while he earned his bachelor's degree at Missouri Southern State University. The same university that his parent's had attended. The same university that James Warren Patrick had attended. James moved to St. Louis to pursue his MBA at Washington University. Ever since, he had felt the need to return home more often than he actually did.

He was becoming well-established in his telecom career when a massive tornado eviscerated Joplin. Amazingly, his parent's home, his grandfather's home, and the Patrick Library were all untouched. But thousands of homes and businesses were completely destroyed. Perhaps it was because his family was spared that James felt such a strong calling to help rebuild the city and restore some sense of normalcy and well-being to the citizens. He spent months in southwest Missouri organizing rebuilding efforts and coordinating community action, long after the mainstream media had forgotten about Joplin.

It was during this time that James began to think about jumping into the political arena. He was disappointed with the inaction of the state and federal agencies that were supposed to help in times of need. Aid money would flow to Joplin, but any real attempts to help would get stifled by bureaucratic red-tape and political inefficiency. Often it was easier to give up than to see an idea come to fruition. This was the first time that he had used his influence as a member of a popular political family to push through initiatives and clear roadblocks. His efforts were well-respected among public, private and political circles throughout the state. That respect served him well when he ran for Governor of Missouri years later.

James was proud of what he was able to accomplish during those months after the tornado, but his fondest memory of that time was meeting Rae. She was an executive with the Red Cross, assigned to coordinate relief efforts in Joplin. The couple first met a few weeks after the disaster and worked closely together for the next several months. James was immediately drawn to her energy, enthusiasm and intellect. Since she had been active in a several disaster recovery efforts through the years, Rae knew what needed to be done. James had the means to help get those things done. They were a powerful team.

Rae was also beautiful. James had noticed her wavy brown hair and captivating brown eyes from the start. He sensed a mutual attraction, but did not act on it until just before Rae was leaving the area for another assignment. They carried on a long-distance relationship, with frequent visits, for a couple of years.

Just before announcing his candidacy for Governor, James took Rae on a weekend get-away. He spent most of the time laying out his strategies, plans and goals for the campaign. Then he told Rae that the only way it would work was if she was by his side. "My life is so much better with you in it," James had said, on bended knee.

Rae accepted, and they were married three months later in the backyard of his parent's house. At the wedding reception, Betty Martin told her new daughter-in-law that she and Joe had known Rae was "the one" the first time they met her, but they had never said anything to their son. "I knew James would figure it out eventually. He always does."

His mother's wedding day comment perfectly summarized the relationship that James had with his parents. They were always available to listen and counsel, but they never meddled. This made it even harder for James to now meddle in their lives. He took some comfort in the fact that his mom had hired a live-in nurse to help with his dad's personal care. The nurse also prepared meals and drove his parents to the doctor and other appointments. James older sister, Deanna Faye, was also close by if needed, yet very busy running the library.

"You could visit them more if they were in D.C.," said Rae. "I would think that would appeal to your mom."

James laughed. "I played that card too. She said she sees more of me now than ever. Every time she turns on the TV, I'm there looking right at her."

"That reminds me," said Rae. "I stopped by to see your fancy new office this afternoon, but Gwen said you were at the Pentagon. I thought you said you would be here all day."

"Duty calls," said James, reaching for the last potato chip before his wife commandeered it as she had the sandwich.

"Couldn't wait to start playing with the Army men, huh?" said Rae, popping the last bite of the sandwich into her mouth.

"Something like that," said James. His mind flashed back to the video and visions of chaos and panic. He remembered the look of horror in Truman's eyes as the former President realized the magnitude of the situation.

After the video, Dennis Gordon and General Bolser had continued to explain the tests and experiments that had been conducted through the years to confirm the theory that the alien device was some type of respirator. In the late 1960s, a research team had been successful in using a complex vacuum system to trap a sample of the deadly substance that was emitted from the device when it was placed into the neck of the alien body. Despite decades of research by some of the world's top chemists, nothing of note had been discovered about the substance, other than the fact that every living thing that was exposed to it died within seconds. "It is easily the deadliest substance on the planet," Dr. Gordon had said.

"Hey," said Rae, fingering James' hair and snapping him back into reality. "You're ignoring me. You must have something really important on your mind."

"Indeed," said James, standing quickly and pulling his wife to her feet. "Dessert. Let's figure out where they keep the cookie jar in this place."

CHAPTER 10

Thursday, January 22, 2037
The White House

Aaron Ash stood beside Gwen Hardin's desk, conferring with the President's secretary. It was 5:30 a.m., still a bit too early for most of the staff, but often the most productive time of the day for Ash.

As Chief Butler, Ash was responsible for the day-to-day administrative operations of the White House, including the President's personal living quarters. This included all aspects of housekeeping, maintenance, grounds keeping and food service. This was a monumental position with enormous responsibility. Ironically, Ash was just under five-feet tall, rotund and balding. Despite his physical stature, he was one of the most respected, and well-known, non-politicians in Washington.

Ash had worked in the White House for 35 years and became Chief Butler 25 years ago. He was revered and admired by his staff for running a tight ship, especially in matters pertaining to the first family and foreign dignitaries visiting the White House. Past Presidents had been so impressed with his people-skills that he had been rumored to have been twice offered positions as a foreign ambassador. Ash would never confirm the stories. He would just simply say, "I have already found my dream job."

At present, he was working with Gwen to find blocks of time during the day that the Oval Office would be vacant. There were a few tasks that still needed to be done inside the office to finalize the transition.

Gwen jotted down times on a scrap of paper. "Keep in mind these times will change as soon as I hand them to you."

"I understand," said Ash. "We will double-check with you before going in. At least we have some times to..." Ash stopped mid-sentence as President Martin stepped into the room from the Oval Office.

"Good morning, sir," said Gwen.

Ash moved toward the hallway. "Excuse me, Mr. President."

"Please. Stay," said Martin moving toward Ash and shaking his hand. "I've been meaning to tell you how nice the office looks. Your staff has done an excellent job."

Ash smiled warmly. "I was just talking with Ms. Hardin about the remaining tasks. The office will be most impressive when everything is complete. I also understand your desk will arrive sometime in February."

"No hurry," said the President. "We've got four years, maybe longer."

Ash laughed. "How about the residence? Are you and Mrs. Martin finding it comfortable?"

"Very," said Martin. "It's exactly as Rae had envisioned it."

"The first lady has excellent taste, Mr. President. Be sure to let me know if you need anything." With a slight bow, Ash turned and left the room.

Martin focused his attention on his secretary. "What is this Gwen? Do you sleep under that desk, or what?"

"Just trying to keep up with you," said Gwen. "I wasn't expecting you until a little after six."

"Couldn't sleep," said Martin. "Day two and I'm already behind."

"Well, sir, get used to it. General Bolser and his crew are already here."

President Martin checked his watch. "They are very early. I'll pop in and surprise them. Green Room, right?"

"No," answered Gwen. "They wanted to spread out a bit so I moved them to W.5.1."

The President looked confused.

"I mean the Roosevelt Room," she explained. "Each room in the White House has a code that is used in the scheduling system. But you don't need to know that."

"I was thinking it would be helpful to put up some signage around here," said Martin. "I made a couple of wrong turns yesterday. I suppose sticking signs on the doors would detract from some of the tradition."

Gwen flashed her wry smile. "Now that you mention it, every door in the building already has a sign on it." She pointed to a small bronze plate attached to the trim above the door leading into the President's office.

Martin approached the door and stood on his tip-toes to get a better view. His eyes widened as he read the plate. "This one says OO.1."

"The rooms located in the West Wing start with W and the East Wing rooms start with E," said Gwen. "The rooms in the original part of the White House all start with M, as in Executive Mansion. The rest of the numbers have something to do with the placement of the rooms. I haven't fully figured that out yet."

"I assume OO stands for Oval Office?" asked the President.

"That's right. It's the only office in the building that does not start with a W, E or M," said Gwen. She was surprised at the President's level of interest in this administrative trivia. "But again, Mr. President, we will always refer to the rooms by their official names."

Martin nodded, now only half-listening to Gwen. He walked back into his office. Shutting the door behind him, he reached inside his pocket for the silver token he had found in the bathroom the previous morning.

"OO.1.2," he muttered to himself as he crossed the room to the main entrance. He opened the door and read the plate that was attached to the trim. *OO.1.* He then checked the plate above the door leading into the Oval Office from his study. It matched the other two doors. He walked back to the center of the room and stood in the middle of the rug bearing the Seal of the President. As he surveyed the office, he noticed two small closet doors set into the long wall on the opposite end of the room. They were the same color and texture as the walls. Both doors blended into the walls so well that they were barely noticeable. He could see the brass plates on the wall above the doors. He moved quickly to the first door. *OO.1.1*

"That's it," said the President, stepping around a wall table toward the second closet. *OO.1.2.*

Martin opened the closet door and stepped into a narrow space just large enough to hold a few stacks of chairs and several flags attached to floor stands. He remembered standing next to the flags yesterday during several photo-ops with various visitors. Behind the flags was a wall, presumably shared with the other closet. He went back to the first closet and checked inside. More chairs and some duct work that appeared to be part of the heating and cooling system.

He closed the closet door and slipped the coin back into his pants pocket.

Spaceships, alien autopsies, codes and closets, thought the President. His first day in office had been more like a movie than a job. He wondered what General Bolser had in store for him this morning. He knew it wouldn't be good, based on what he saw yesterday, and the fact that they had yet to explain the importance of August.

CHAPTER 11

Thursday, January 22, 2037
The White House

General Bolser and another uniformed man bolted upright from their chairs as the President entered the Roosevelt Room. It was obvious, from the documents scattered around the table, they had been working for some time. This was impressive considering the fact it was just before 6 a.m.

"Mr. President," said the General, reaching for his jacket which was draped across the chair. "Good morning. We weren't expecting you for a while."

"Sit back down gentlemen," said Martin, removing his own jacket. "Let's forgo the formalities. It's the least I can do for getting you up so early."

The younger man took his seat then looked horribly confused when he noticed that General Bolser had remained standing. Bolser placed his jacket back on the chair. "We were just finalizing your briefing, Mr. President."

The President took a seat across the table from the two men. "I'm not looking for a polished presentation, General. You got my attention yesterday. I want to know more about August."

"There is a strong possibility that the aliens are coming back around August of this year, Mr. President," said Bolser, reaching for a large envelope as he returned to his seat.

Bolser removed another grey metallic sheet, similar to the one he had presented in the Oval Office the day before. He slid the sheet across the table to the President. "The sheet you saw yesterday had a number of indecipherable symbols and markings. This one contains a map-like representation of a portion of our solar system, as well as several nearby systems. Take a look at the center of the sheet."

Martin examined the sheet, noting the same purple haze that emitted from the grey metal to form symbols and markings. A dark dot, about the size of a dime, glowed from the middle of the page. The dot was surrounded by four circles, each larger than the one before. Each circle had a dark dot somewhere on its perimeter. The dots varied in size, but were all much smaller than the center dot.

"This does look like a solar system," said the President. "But it can't be ours, there aren't enough planets."

"I'm going to ask Kyle Lakey to explain how we know for certain that is our solar system," said Bolser, motioning to the young man. "Dr. Lakey is on loan to the Majestic project from NASA."

"Good morning, Mr. President," said Lakey. "The center dot is our sun. The four circles represent the orbits of the first four planets in our solar system. The smaller dots on the circles are: Mercury, Venus, Earth and Mars. We know this because the location of each dot on each circle represents their exact position in orbit."

The President considered Lakey's statement. "Do you mean the positions of their orbits in 1946?"

"No, sir. Their positions as of today," said Lakey. "The dots move. Under extreme magnification we have been able to prove that the dots are constantly in motion, similar to the actual planets. This movement is imperceptible to the naked eye, but if you look at the sheet every few days the movement is obvious. Each dot moves in exact time with the planet's orbit."

"And they have been moving like this for ninety years?" asked Martin.

"Yes, sir," said Lakey. "The scientists noticed this shortly after the sheets were recovered from the crash site."

"What about all of the other circles and dots on the sheet?" asked the President. "Are these other solar systems?"

Lakey nodded. "Yes. The center dots are suns; 17 of them in all. Each is surrounded by at least one planet. Some are orbited by as many as 10. All of the dots, or planets, move constantly, just like the dots in the center solar system. Based on the orbits of the various planets, we have been able to associate each solar system represented on this sheet with a known solar system in our universe. Sixteen of them are within our own Milky Way galaxy."

Lakey leaned across the table and pointed to a set of circles in the top right corner of the sheet. "This one is part of Canis Major."

"You just lost me," said the President, picking up the sheet and examining the circles. "Canis Major?"

The young scientist shifted eagerly in his chair. "It's a neighboring galaxy that was discovered around the turn of the century. This solar system is located on the edge of Canis Major that is closest to the Milky Way."

"How close?" said Martin.

"About 25,000 light years," answered Lakey.

The President laughed. "We call that a neighboring galaxy?"

"In the cosmic scheme of things, 25,000 light years is pretty close," explained Lakey. "Much closer if you factor in means of transportation beyond our known realities."

"Now you have really lost me," said Martin.

General Bolser chimed in. "We were finalizing some visuals to help explain some of these concepts, Mr. President."

President Martin raised his hand. "Let's stick with the verbal version for now, General. Dr. Lakey has been pretty clear thus far."

"If you only consider what we might call *normal* time and distance, something that is 25,000 light years away is well beyond our reach," continued Lakey. "But many speculate that time and distance is not consistent throughout the universe. Things like worm holes and black holes alter matter. They could very well alter time and distance as well."

Martin nodded. "You're talking about the theory that you could enter a worm hole on one side of the universe and come out on the other side of the universe."

Lakey nodded.

"Isn't that just science fiction?" asked Martin.

"It's mostly been presented as sci-fi," agreed Lakey. "But it's based on real theories, which are based on solid science."

"What science?" asked the President.

"You're holding it," said Lakey. "Astronomers in 2003 discovered Canis Major because of something we saw on that sheet."

"What was that?" asked Martin.

"One of the dots in that corner solar system disappeared," said Lakey. "Prior to March 2002 there were three dots, or planets, orbiting that sun. Then the middle planet just disappeared. So did the circle representing its orbit. Because the structures of the solar systems and the orbits of the planets on this sheet were so accurate, scientists knew this disappearing dot was significant. At the time that dot disappeared from the sheet, we had no idea where the corner solar system was located. We just knew it wasn't in our galaxy. The disappearing dot gave us a hint. We assumed it represented a catastrophic event; one that would have to have been extremely violent to result in the complete destruction of a planet.

"Astronomers focused on an area of space just beyond our galaxy that was known to be very unstable. After several months of study they found Canis Major tucked behind a section of the Milky Way that is extremely dense. Canis Major is a small galaxy that is being pulled apart due to the gravitational pull of the Milky Way. Years of catalogued data from deep-space telescopes and other monitoring devices enabled the team to pinpoint the solar system, along with the former location of the missing planet, on the edge of the newly found galaxy."

"Ok," said the President, tapping the corner of the metallic sheet with a pen. "This alien artifact leads to the discovery of a previously unknown galaxy. But I don't understand how we extend that to interstellar space travel."

Lakey reached for the sheet. "Another intriguing aspect of the Canis Major solar system is the fact that it has never moved. This corner solar system, and ours in the middle of the sheet, has never moved. For years, people working on Majestic referred to the corner solar system as *Anchor* and our solar system as *Target*. We theorize that our solar system stays static at the center of the sheet because it represents their destination. It would follow that the corner solar system is static because it represents the point of origin."

"So the anchor and target don't move, but the other solar systems do?" asked Martin.

"Very infrequently, but yes they do," said Lakey. "Not far, but enough to notice on the sheet."

"What does the movement represent?" asked Martin.

"Great question," said Lakey. "That's where the black holes come into play. Black holes thrive in unstable areas of space. Like around the Canis Major galaxy. They also move around quite a bit. We have noticed that movements of some of the solar systems on this sheet correspond with the movement of black holes around the edge of our galaxy, near Canis Major.

"If the worm hole theorists are correct, you could enter a black hole in Canis Major and exit somewhere in the Milky Way. These holes are known to be unstable, which explains why the exit point would change. If the aliens had the ability to analyze and chart the changes in the worm holes, they could use them efficiently for travel."

"I thought a black hole destroyed everything around it," said Martin.

General Bolser responded. "That is the common belief. But we've not been able to put the slightest scratch on anything taken from the crash site. We are dealing with something very advanced, both in terms of knowledge and technology."

"But if they are using these worm hole expressways, wouldn't there have to be an exit ramp somewhere close to the Earth?" asked the President. "There are no black holes near the Earth."

"True," said Bolser. "We speculate that the aliens may have only needed to travel the great distance between their galaxy and ours once. In fact, the Canis Major galaxy is so unstable that they may not be able to return. It's even possible the planet that disappeared in 2003 was their home planet."

"So they are just stuck out there flying around in space?" asked Martin.

"Yes and no," answered the General. "We believe they have found a temporary home, one that provides both transportation and some level of protection. Dr. Lakey, could you elaborate?"

"Certainly," said Lakey, sliding the metallic sheet back towards the President and pointing at the center. "You may have noticed this thin arcing line near the circle that represents the Earth's orbit. This is the current trajectory of an asteroid named 29075 DA. It was discovered in 1950."

President Martin fingered the sheet. "Let me guess. The asteroid was found based on clues from this little beauty."

"That's right," said Lakey. "The location of the arc on Earth's orbit, coupled with its proximity to Mars, pointed astronomers right to it. It's a little more than a kilometer in diameter, which is pretty small compared to other asteroids, so it had been overlooked previously."

"And they are using this rock as some kind of space base?" asked Martin.

"That is our belief," said General Bolser. He retrieved another metallic sheet from his briefcase and slid it across the table to the President. "This will help explain things."

Martin studied the new sheet. It was the same size and color as the previous sheets. This one displayed an image of a rock that seemed to almost hover above the sheet, giving it a 3D-type effect.

"This is a model of the 29075 DA asteroid," said Bolser.

The detail of the image was amazing. As the President rotated the sheet, the topography of the asteroid's surface shifted to reveal mountain peaks, plateaus and ravines.

"Touch one of the mountains, Mr. President," said Bolser.

Martin ran an index finger across the peak of one of the mountain ranges. The image expanded outward from the sheet, providing a larger and more detailed view of the area surrounding the mountain. The flat surface at the base of the mountain now showed several clusters of structures. He touched one of the structures, the image shifted to a detailed view of the surface revealing groups of spacecraft, the same shape as the model he had seen at the pentagon yesterday.

"This reminds me of a satellite model of a military complex," said the President.

"That's a good analogy, sir," said Bolser. "The craft move around on occasion, which make us believe that this is a real-time view of the asteroid, similar to the orbits of the planets on the other sheet. There are also a number of larger craft which move more frequently."

"How do we know we are looking at the asteroid?" asked Martin. "Maybe this is their home planet."

"That's what was assumed until 29075 DA was discovered," said the General. "Once we mapped the surface of the asteroid, we realized it was exactly the same as this model."

Lakey motioned toward the sheet and added, "Plus, the proximity of the arc on the sheet matches the current path the asteroid is traveling through the solar system."

"What do you mean by current?" asked Martin.

"That's where this really gets weird," said Lakey. "The astronomer that discovered 29075 DA in 1950 observed it for 17 days. Then it disappeared."

"Is it normal for asteroids to disappear?" asked the President. "Did it just go behind another planet or the sun?"

Lakey inched forward excitedly in his chair. "No, sir. It completely disappeared. And at the same time, the arc on this sheet moved from our solar system to Canis Major."

Martin thought for a moment. "So it...passed back through the worm hole?"

"Exactly," said Lakey.

"Did the spacecraft stay on the asteroid when it was in Canis Major?" asked Martin.

"Just a few of them," said Bolser. "We think the rest of them returned to their home planet."

"And they stayed there for about 50 years, until the middle of 2000, when we noticed an increase in the number of spacecraft on the asteroid," said Lakey. "Nothing much happened until December 28, 2000 when the arc moved back to the section of the sheet representing our solar system."

"Were the astronomers then able to see it again?" asked Martin.

"Yes," said Lakey. "The interesting part about that is those astronomers were not part of the Majestic project. They were independent researchers from all over the planet that said the asteroid just appeared out of nowhere. It was years before they realized it was 29075 DA."

The President studied the sheet for another moment. "How often does the asteroid move between the solar systems?"

"It has not moved back," said Lakey. "It's been in our solar system since the end of 2000."

"Wasn't that about the time the planet disappeared from Canis Major?" asked Martin.

"Yes," said Lakey.

"They might have been escaping from a doomed planet," said Martin.

Bolser and Lakey answered in unison. "That's right."

Martin tapped the arc with his finger. "Based on this, they are getting pretty close to Earth."

Bolser leaned forward and sighed. "They are very close, sir. In fact, they will pass within a few hundred thousand miles of this planet in. . ."

"August," interrupted Martin.

Bolser nodded.

Martin slid the sheet across the table to Bolser. "This just keeps getting better."

There was a sharp rap on the door as Alan Kingman and Secretary Knudsen entered the room.

"You guys didn't start without us did you?" said Kingman.

"I had to have a little sneak peek," said Martin, checking his watch and reaching for his jacket. "I have a few other matters to attend to this morning. Otherwise they are going to dock my pay for skipping meetings. Dr. Lakey, you and General Bolser take these two through what you just showed me. Don't worry about the fancy presentations. I'll be back this afternoon. I assume you have even more to tell me."

General Bolser was standing at attention again. "Yes, sir. There is more."

Martin smiled at Kingman and Knudsen as he left the room. "Try to have this resolved before I get back."

CHAPTER 12

Thursday, January 22, 2037
The White House

President Martin sat at his desk in the Oval Office enjoying a brief moment of quiet. His morning and early afternoon had been filled with non-stop meetings: more introductions, and briefings, and budgets. All of this was good information, and he had managed to remain focused, but he needed to be back in the Roosevelt Room.

It was just after two o'clock. He had asked Gwen to push his final two meetings back 15 minutes to give him some time alone. He eyed the closet door from across the room, and then glanced at the clock on the desk. *2:04.*

Martin rose from his seat and slowly walked toward the closet. He read the bronze plate above the door again. *OO.1.2.* He opened the door and stepped in amidst the chairs and flags, working his way along the wall toward the inner-most wall.

He pulled back one of the flags and noticed that the fabric was much heavier than the other flags. His eyes widened as he moved first his head, and then his body, beyond the cloth into a small dimly lit room. He turned to look back into the closet but found only a wall and a floor length tapestry where the flag had been.

Martin blinked repeatedly as he turned back to face the room. There was a small window on the far wall, two tables, a reading lamp, and a dusty dry fireplace. Everything was the same color, a sandy light brown. As his eyes adjusted, he noticed more furniture and knick-knacks. He was in a living room of some sort.

He turned again and pulled back the tapestry. This time, he closed his eyes hard, assuming that he was dreaming. He was ready to wake up.

"Welcome, Mr. President. You are right on time."

Martin opened his eyes and turned toward the voice. He saw the back of a chair in the middle of the room. He was certain it had not been there before because it blocked his view of the fireplace, which was now burning with a crackling brown flame, the same color as the rest of the room.

The chair began to rotate. A man rose and stepped toward him. He was several inches shorter than Martin and much thinner. He was dressed in an out-dated suit that appeared to be a size too large. The suit, along with his shoes, his skin and his thinning hair, were the same neutral tone as the rest of the room. He blended in perfectly, except for the sharp steel blue eyes which bugged out a bit from his gaunt sunken face.

"It is a pleasure to meet you, sir. Thank you for coming."

Martin was speechless and unable to move. He stared at the man. The man quietly stared back, blinking every few seconds.

The fireplace crackled again. The man blinked.

Crackle, blink, *crackle*, blink...

"Are you one of them?" asked Martin, his voice barely audible, his eyes unyielding.

"One of whom?" the man replied.

"One of them," said Martin. "The aliens."

"No," said the man. "I am not one of them. I am one of you."

Crackle, blink.

"Why are you here?" asked Martin.

"I am here because you are here. Would you like to sit down?" the man motioned toward a second chair. Like the first, it was a small padded armchair with a flared back. And like the first, Martin was certain it had not been there when he first entered the room.

65

"What do you want?" asked Martin without moving. His voice was stronger now, with a hint of impatience.

"I wanted to let you know that I am here to help you."

"Help me with what?"

"With anything you wish, Mr. President."

Martin thought for a moment, then broke eye-contact with the man and glanced around the room again. His eyes had fully adjusted to the darkness, and things were clearer now. Still dull and brown, but clearer.

"Who else knows you are here?" asked Martin.

The man shifted and smiled. His eyes widened even more. "Oh I suspect they all know I'm here."

Martin was growing increasingly frustrated with the conversation and increasingly uncomfortable with the surroundings. He stepped back toward the wall and reached for the tapestry, still staring at the man.

"Please come again, any time," said the man, with a slight bow and a longer blink.

This time Martin noticed a deeper space behind the tapestry. He turned to step into the shadow, then looked back at the man. "What do I call you?"

"Call me by name," said the man. "Mortimer."

"Mortimer," repeated Martin.

The man nodded.

CHAPTER 13

President Martin stood in the middle of the Oval Office, halfway between his desk and the small closet from which he had just exited. He was torn between the urge to return to the closet and the need to get back to work. Better yet, maybe he should go home and go to bed.

I must be going out of my mind, he thought. *Aliens are riding bareback on asteroids. And now there's a little man setting up residence between the walls in the White House.*

He heard the crackle again. Spinning toward the fireplace he realized it was the speaker on his desk.

"Mr. President," said Gwen. "Mr. Kingman would like a moment with you if possible"

Martin walked around the desk and checked the clock. It changed from 2:05 to 2:06 as he sat down.

"Impossible." muttered Martin. He looked at his watch.

"Excuse me, sir?" said Gwen.

The President took a deep breath, determined to return to his senses. "Send him in Gwen."

Seconds later Alan Kingman entered the office and walked quickly toward the desk. His hair was tussled, his eyes bleary from hours of intense discussions with General Bolser and the Majestic staff.

"I didn't think this could get any weirder," said Kingman. "I was wrong. Way wrong."

"You mean the asteroid," said Martin.

"That's just the start," said Kingman, sliding one of the grey alien sheets from an envelope. "You saw this asteroid model this morning, right?"

President Martin ran a finger across one of the mountain peaks and again surveyed the rows of Hecatian craft. "Yes, I was looking at this just before you and Knudsen arrived."

Kingman reached across the desk and touched the peak of the highest rock formations on the model. Then he turned the sheet to bring the formation closer to the President. "Look at the top of this rock."

Martin moved closer. "Looks like some kind of building with a satellite dish or something on top of it; maybe a communications center?"

Kingman shook his head. "Take another look at the shape of that thing on top of the building."

Martin turned the sheet a few inches. "It looks like one of those respirators Dr. Gordon showed us at the Pentagon yesterday. Based on the scale of this model, this one is huge."

"So are these," said Kingman, as he touched the tops of four other rocky bluffs. Similar buildings, each supporting a large version of the respirator, were revealed. A light purple grid appeared, connecting each of the respirators. This formed the illusion of a roof over the entire colony.

"What have they done?" asked Martin. "Create their own atmosphere?"

"Exactly," answered Kingman. "They have constructed giant respirators at the highest points on the asteroid. Bolser says all of their activity takes place within the boundaries of that grid. They must be pretty powerful because there are thousands of feet between those bluffs."

"Based on what we saw on that video yesterday, we wouldn't want to get anywhere near that rock," said Martin. "That must be why Bolser is so worried about August. Does he think the asteroid will pass close enough to affect our atmosphere?"

Kingman shook his head and took out another grey sheet from the envelope. "Yes and no. It's not the asteroid that has them worried."

Sliding the asteroid model to the side, Kingman placed the new grey sheet in front of the President and tapped the middle. A flat map of Earth appeared with the continents glowing in various hues of silver and purple. Kingman touched North America and the map adjusted focus. North American grew in size and rose up from the sheet providing a three-dimensional view.

"Let's test your memory of junior high geography," said Kingman. "What's the highest point in the continental United States?"

"That would be Mt. Whitney in California," said Martin.

"Correct," said Kingman, touching the center of California. Mt. Whitney rose from the sheet. "Followed by?"

Martin shook his head and grinned. "I have no clue."

"Me either," said Kingman. "Prior to today, I couldn't have named more than a couple of mountains in the US. But thanks to General Bolser," he touched several places on the map. "Mt. Elbert in Colorado, Rainier in Washington, Gannett Peak Wyoming, Mt. Hood in Oregon."

As he continued to work the map, peaks rose from the metallic sheet. Purple icons in the shape of the respirator appeared above each peak. When Kingman was finished a grid, similar to the one on the asteroid model, formed over a large portion of the northwest quarter of the United States. It stretched from the Rockies to the Pacific and from southern Canada to New Mexico.

"So they intend to annex some of our land," said Martin, leaning back in his chair and running his hands through his hair.

"Most of our land," said Kingman. "Actually, most of our planet."

He lifted the metallic sheet and tapped the side. The flat map transformed into translucent globe which hovered above the desk. The image of Earth was about the size of a beach ball. As Kingman rotated the model, several of the purple grids glowed across North America, Europe, Asia, Africa and the Middle East.

"It appears they have lofty goals," said Kingman. "And I don't think we're part of the plan."

CHAPTER 14

Thursday, January 22, 2037
Washington, D.C.

It was mid-afternoon, just late enough for the winter sun to have dipped below the tree-line casting shadows across the office. Rudolph Overton considered turning on the desk lamp, but the glow from his laptop provided sufficient light. The younger members of the staff often teased him because he still used a laptop. He grinned to himself. Hell, they were *all* younger members of the staff, especially compared to him.

He had never married. He had no kids or family to speak of. His lifelong lack of social interaction made him an unknown among the Washington elite. At the same time, his work ethic and ambition was well-known, perhaps legendary, throughout the Capitol. Overton had no time for nonsense. Early in his career, through tireless effort, he had positioned himself as one of the top import/export and shipping magnates in the world. He had traveled the globe, many times over, amassing a personal fortune. He took a huge pay cut when he joined the Federal Trade Commission in the 1990s, eventually working his way to the top spot. He had spent decades working at 600 Pennsylvania Ave. Not the most powerful address on the street, but not far from it.

Though no one knew for sure, it was assumed that Overton was somewhere in his late 80s. It was difficult to estimate his age based on appearance. Not because he had aged gracefully, rather because he had always looked old. Tall and slender, Overton had a thin head of combed-back hair, not quite blonde and not quite grey. His eyes were his most striking feature, bluish/grey, like ocean fog. They were intense and always seemed to be looking into the distance, as if searching for something.

71

Overton was now just a just a figurehead at the FTC, but he still earned a salary mentoring the up-and-comers and consulting with key nations and international companies. With his official duties significantly reduced, he was free to resume activities with some of his global shipping interests. He still maintained an office, but had given up his staff years ago. He preferred to handle his own scheduling and correspondence.

He liked the way the darkening room enhanced the video on his screen. Asteroid 29075 DA had moved close enough to the Earth to be in range of NASA's long-range telescopes. Over the past few weeks, NASA had posted photos, and even some short videos, of the space rock on their public website.

He could tell from the lack of inane comments on the asteroid page that he was among a few handful of people who had bothered to view the photos and videos. Not surprising. 29075 DA was just one of thousands of asteroids being tracked by NASA. And while it was expected to intersect Earth's orbit later in the year, it would still be 100,000 miles from the planet.

Just another benign chunk of rock hurtling harmlessly through the cosmos, he murmured to himself and unlocked one of the desk drawers. He carefully removed the object that he had brought from home that morning. This object rarely left his home. In fact, it rarely left the worn wooden box that adorned the desk in the study of his residence. But things were moving quickly now and he needed the object close by at all times.

Overton's pulse quickened. He ran a long withered finger across the series of glowing purple dots and circles. *No,* he thought, *not benign. And far from harmless.* He knew better. He knew the truth. And he had been waiting for this truth to return for a very, very long time.

CHAPTER 15

President Martin stood on the patio, just outside the Oval Office, looking out into the Rose Garden. Chris Boone and a second agent were positioned along a covered walkway that led to the residence section of the White House.

Late January in D.C. was still a long way from garden weather, but Martin found the cold air invigorating. It cleared his mind and provided a degree of calm.

Kingman had returned to the Roosevelt Room to wrap-up the day's activities with the Generals and the Majestic team. According to General Bolser, all of the major surprises and storylines pertaining to the Hecatians had been revealed. There was still much to review over the coming weeks, but what remained was merely supporting information to the horrifying facts that had been presented over the past two days.

The Roswell conspiracy theories of the second half of the 20th century were true. An alien race existed, one that planned to invade and inhabit this planet. All indications were that they were set to return in just a few months.

Martin took another gulp of the cold air. He thought about the other Presidents who had stood on this patio, perhaps contemplating the same issue. No wonder Rosemont had practically sprinted away from a second term in office. He couldn't blame him. No one in their right mind would want to deal with this.

The President returned to his office, closing the glass door behind him. As he turned toward his desk, his eye caught a shadow moving just beyond the door to the private study and dining room.

He was certain that door had been closed when he was meeting with Kingman, and he had left via the door to Gwen's office.

Martin moved cautiously toward the half open door.

"Who's there?" he demanded.

The shadow shifted. The door opened wider.

"I'm sorry, Mr. President," answered a gravelly voice. "It's just me, sir. Townsend."

The name was familiar, but the voice was not. Martin took a step closer to the door. A lanky black man with close-cropped grey hair stepped through the door. He was dressed in a black and white steward's suit, sans jacket. He was wearing white gloves and nervously pulled at the suspenders which lay across the front of his pristine white shirt.

"Ah yes," said Martin, relief evident in his voice. "Milford Townsend, the keeper of the office."

"Yes, sir, Mr. President," replied Townsend. "I didn't realize you were still here."

"No worries, Mr. Townsend. I've been meaning to say hello. It's been pretty crazy around here the past couple of days. I haven't been able to make the rounds yet."

Martin extended a hand. "I understand you trump everyone here in terms of tenure."

Townsend quickly removed his right glove and shook hands with the President. "I believe so, sir, a little over 60 years."

"And all right here in the Oval Office?" asked Martin, returning to his desk.

"Yes, sir," answered Townsend with a nod and a proud smile. "I must say that it's really nice to see that desk again."

"Just for a few weeks, but I agree, it seemed like the right thing to do."

Townsend took a step closer. "Someone's been taking real good care of it. It looks as good as when your grandpa sat behind it."

"Tell me how you ended up working with my grandfather."

"I was the beneficiary of President Patrick's good graces," Townsend said, his distinct southern drawl grew more prominent. "My daddy had worked the Oval Office just about his whole life, going all the way back to President Truman. I had just turned 18 when he died. He had got me a job downstairs cleaning the kitchen. When I came back to work a few days after Dad's funeral, President Patrick called me up to this office. He said he thought the job should stay in the family, and that I could have it if I wanted it."

Martin smiled. "Sounds like the job worked out for you."

"Yes, sir," agreed Townsend. "I had decided it was about time for me to retire a few years back. Then it began to look like you would be coming here. I figured I should stick around a little longer."

President Martin stood from his chair with a laugh. "I'm glad you made that decision, Mr. Townsend. It's good knowing you are here."

"Please, everyone just calls me Townsend around here. If you need anything, just let Ms. Harding or Mr. Ash know. I'll get right on it."

The two men walked back toward the door that led to the dining room. Martin stopped short, eyeing the closet doors.

"I've been wondering about these closets, Townsend. What do you keep in there beside chairs and flags?"

The steward thought for a moment. "Sometimes we stick the photo equipment in there. But we don't use them much. They have only been there a few years. I guess we don't think about them."

"What do you mean they've only been there a few years?" asked Martin.

"They put them in when President Rosemont had the fireplace removed."

Moments later Townsend departed, closing the door behind him. President Martin stood between the closet doors looking at the wall table where the fireplace had been. How could he have missed

that? He had seen hundreds of pictures of his grandfather in this office. The fireplace was in the background of many of those photos.

Why would Rosemont want the fireplace removed?

Martin looked at the closet door.

CHAPTER 16

Thursday, January 22, 2037
The White House

Martin reached for the farthest flag, this time stretching it out in front of him. It was too dark to tell what color it was, but it was definitely a flag. It was attached to a pole which was standing in a metal base plate. Martin toed the base plate and let the flag drop.

Crackle.

He stepped forward and felt the heavy tapestry drop behind him. He was in the same room with the same drab color everywhere. The brown fireplace was roaring. He looked down. A few feet in front of him sat a short-haired cat, brown with bulging blue eyes. Martin stepped closer. The cat's face had an uncanny resemblance to the man he had met here that afternoon.

Crackle.

Martin turned toward the fireplace. At that instant, the cat jumped backward with a slight yelp and landed in the lap of Mortimer, who was sitting in his chair, dressed as he was previously. Mortimer remained seated. He and the cat both stared at Martin, both blinking their big blue eyes in unison.

"Mortimer was it?" said Martin.

"Indeed, Mr. President, I am Mortimer. How can I help you?"

Martin spun quickly, grabbing the tapestry with one hand and feeling along the wall with the other. He pulled on the material and noticed that it was attached to a rod that ran along the ceiling. He turned back toward Mortimer.

Mortimer blinked. The cat blinked. The fireplace crackled.

"You want to help me?" said Martin.

"I would be most happy to help you, Mr. President."

"Then answer a question."

Mortimer nodded.

"Am I dreaming?" asked Martin.

"No," replied Mortimer.

"Are you real?"

"I am as real as you." Mortimer's eyes widened.

Martin surveyed the room. It was as he remembered from his first visit. His eyes had adjusted to the dim light. He looked back at Mortimer and thought for a moment.

"Did you know President Rosemont?" he asked.

"I know everyone," answered Mortimer.

"Did he visit you?"

"Not like this. He was more resistant."

"Resistant to what?"

"To this," said Mortimer.

Martin sighed, shook his head and looked down. "I feel like I'm in the middle of a Dr. Seuss book."

Mortimer smiled. "This can be puzzling. But with time it becomes clearer."

Martin looked again at the fireplace. It roughly matched the style that he remembered from the pictures.

"Do you know why Rosemont had the fireplace removed?" asked Martin.

"I do not know for sure," said Mortimer. "But I suspect it had something to do with his resistance."

"It was because he was a worthless pain in the tookus!" said a voice, slightly higher pitched than Mortimer's.

Mortimer closed his eyes and shook his head slowly. "I thought we agreed you would stay out of this for the time being."

A chair, which was an exact match to Mortimer's, and one that Martin was certain had not been there moments before, rotated to face the President. Seated in the chair was a woman. Perhaps a twin. She was significantly plumper than Mortimer, but with the same blue bulging eyes. Her rumpled house dress was the same dusty color as the rest of the surroundings.

Again, Martin found himself speechless. He looked first at the woman, and then back at Mortimer, then finally at the cat. It was obvious that his three hosts did not find this encounter the least bit unusual. They were patiently waiting for him to catch-up, blinking all the while. First Mortimer, then the woman, then the cat, and then the three of them in unison.

"Me-oh-my he's a talkative one isn't he." said the woman.

"Emma, some restraint please," said Mortimer. "Mr. President, may I present Emma?"

Martin nodded slightly, more out of habit than anything else. "Ma'am."

"Ah, manners!" said Emma, her eyes brightening. "How refreshing. You don't see good manners much nowadays. Why I remember when people would..."

"Emma," interrupted Mortimer, his voice firm, but still calm. "Perhaps you should consider *your* manners?"

The woman glared at Mortimer, letting out a slight snort which sent the cat scrambling for cover under the chair. "I wasn't talking to you, you crotchety old fart. I was just about to offer our guest some coffee."

She turned her gaze back toward the President. "How about some coffee dear?"

"No, I'm fine," said Martin.

"Nonsense," said Emma, rising from her chair and shuffling past the fireplace toward another room, mumbling something else about manners. The cat emerged from under the chair and trotted after the woman. Its stubby tail was wagging furiously.

Martin watched intently until the cat rounded the corner. That tail seemed out of place. In fact, he was pretty sure that cat had a long furry tail earlier. Maybe it was a different cat, one with a stubby tail that wagged, like a dog. No, it was too small to be a dog.

Perhaps a puppy. Martin rubbed his eyes, trying desperately to wake-up. He looked again at Mortimer, who was still seated. Calm, comfortable, blinking.

"You were saying that Rosemont had the fireplace removed because of some type of reluctance?" said Martin.

Mortimer shook his head. "I said resistance, but he was reluctant as well."

"He was an ass," corrected Emma. She had returned to her chair. Despite being gone for just a few seconds, she had managed to arrange a full coffee service on a recently-appearing table between herself and Mortimer. The coffee had already been poured into three china cups which were sitting on matching saucers. Emma stared eagerly at Martin, as did the pup, or rather the cat, which was now sitting in her lap.

Pup, or cat, thought Martin. *Puppercat*, that would work.

"Do sit down, Mr. President," offered Mortimer, with a glance at the chair that had appeared next to Martin.

Martin sat.

"Now we're making progress," said Mortimer. He picked up a small container from the table. "Cream, Mr. President?"

"Thank you," said Martin. He watched as Mortimer poured a dash of cream into each of the steaming cups. Martin reached for a napkin and his coffee, and then paused.

"Something wrong?" asked Emma.

"Just looking for a spoon," answered Martin.

"Whatever for?" asked Emma, as if this were the most unusual request she had ever heard.

Martin hesitated. "To stir the coffee," he said, making his statement sound more like a question.

"Oh, we don't stir," said Emma, with a hint of superiority. She looked briefly, almost lovingly, at Mortimer. "We're swirlers."

"Swirlers?" said Martin, shifting his attention to Mortimer who was holding a saucer with two hands and gazing intently at his coffee.

"Indeed," said Mortimer. "Let the cream work its way through the coffee on its own. This gives you time to contemplate."

Martin looked into his cup. The same shades of brown and tan that had filled the room were now circling in the black liquid. The same tan as Mortimer's suit and Emma's dress. The same brown as the chairs and the puppercat. The steam reached his face just as the fireplace crackled.

"Contemplate what?" asked Martin, without looking up.

"Whatever needs contemplating," said Mortimer. "Sometimes we just need to pause and focus long enough to find our vision."

"And sometimes you just need to pause long enough for the coffee to cool off so you don't burn your lips," Emma added.

Mortimer and Martin both broke their coffee gaze and looked at Emma. She was taking turns sipping at and blowing on her coffee. Sip. Blow. Sip. Blow. She stopped when she noticed their stares.

"What?" said Emma.

"Why do you insist on interrupting every thought we have?" said Mortimer, returning his cup and saucer to the table.

"I'm just saying that hot coffee can burn your lips," answered Emma. "That's really more of an observation than an interruption."

CHAPTER 17

It was very early, but there were still several staff members and aides bustling about as President Martin walked briskly along the corridor that connected the White House residence with the West Wing. Martin exchanged greetings with several staffers as he passed through to the Oval Office.

"Welcome back, Mr. President," Gwen Hardin greeted him at his office door.

Martin smiled. "I sure am glad to see you again Gwen. Nothing ever runs as smoothly when you're not around. From now on, I want you with me on every trip."

"Not a chance, Mr. President," Gwen said dryly.

Martin feigned surprise. "Come on. Air Force One, five-star hotels."

"Not a chance, Mr. President." Gwen repeated as she motioned the President into his office. "There's plenty to do around here."

The President had spent the last six days jetting around the globe on his first official overseas trip. There were dignitaries to meet, speeches to give, relationships to make or mend.

In the weeks leading up to the trip, Martin had tried to focus on the day-to-day activities of governing a nation. The role of President would be overwhelming to any person. Add to all of this the alien invasion issue that was ever-present in the back of his mind. Martin already felt like he had been on the job for a year. In reality, it was just February.

Martin had resisted the temptation to revisit the Oval Office closet. That was yet another odd circumstance that he needed to resolve. He glanced toward the closet as he and Gwen entered the room. Something was different.

He turned and surveyed the rest of the office…freshly painted walls. "Now this really looks nice."

"Yes it does," said Gwen. "And it gets better." She was standing behind his desk; his new desk. "Rudolph Ash worked some magic with the Arnalls and the shipping company. It was delivered late last night."

Martin circled the desk slowly taking in the craftsmanship and the attention to detail. It was magnificent. Despite its perfect polish and unblemished surface, it looked like it had graced the Oval Office for decades.

"This is perfect," said the President, lowering himself into his chair. "I knew it would be nice, but this is…" His thoughts shifted to a memory of his grandfather sitting at his desk in the same office. He remembered how special he felt when he got to visit Papa in his big office. He remembered sitting in his lap. He could still feel the hugs. He felt tears coming.

"I'd like to phone Dean Arnall later this morning," he said, as he tested the desk drawers. Each was already filled with the contents from the previous desk.

"I transferred the things from your Grandfather's desk this morning," said Gwen. "You will want to check the middle drawer."

Martin slid his chair back and opened the lap drawer. He removed a flat cardboard box. He read the message that was written across the top of the package. *"We had some extra wood. – D. Arnall"*

He opened the box and slid out a wooden picture frame. The wood was walnut and stained the exact shade as the desk. Behind the glass was a color photo of a young boy clutching the tip of an American flag.

"My goodness," said Gwen. "That picture has certainly come full-circle."

83

The President shook his head in disbelief. He had considered displaying this photo in the Oval Office when he moved in, but decided against it, thinking it might be a distraction for visitors. It was unlikely that there was a person on the planet who had not seen this picture. It ran in every newspaper and magazine during the days following his grandfather's funeral. Along with the photo of JFK Jr. saluting his father's coffin in 1963, this image of a six-year-old James Patrick Martin adjusting the flag on his grandfather's front porch was among the most famous and beloved presidential photos.

He placed the framed photo next to a picture of Rae on the bureau behind his chair.

"You have a few minutes at 10:15 this morning," said Gwen. "I'll have Mr. Arnall on the phone for you then."

"Thanks," said Martin. "Be sure to tell Mr. Ash how much I appreciate his efforts to get this all done."

A few moments after exiting the Oval Office, Gwen was back with Alan Kingman in tow.

"Welcome back," said Kingman. "Did you get any sleep?"

"Enough," said Martin. He motioned to the couch in the middle of the room. Both men sat. Kingman reached for the coffee and poured two cups.

"I'm concerned about General Knudsen," said Kingman, wasting no time in getting down to business.

"How so?" said Martin.

Kingman sipped his coffee. "He's obsessed with the Majestic issue. I mean, I know we're all obsessed with this, but his focus is solely militaristic. Hell, we haven't even made it to Mars yet and he's talking about nuking asteroids."

"Do you know what caused him to head in that direction?" asked Martin.

"Assuming it wasn't you," Kingman paused.

The President shook his head.

"Then, I have no idea. It definitely wasn't Bolser. He's way beyond considering any type of armed heroics."

Martin was staring into his coffee cup. The cream was still swirling. "Bolser and Knudsen are both soldiers. It's natural for a soldier to think about shooting first. Bolser's just had more time to mull this over."

"We can't fight and we can't flee," said Kingman. "What's left?"

"I don't know," said Martin. "I think it might be time to get some other opinions on our options."

Kingman raised an eyebrow. "Like who?"

"Like everyone's," said the President.

CHAPTER 18

Later that morning, President Martin was seated behind his new desk sifting through a series of virtual papers. Two IT technicians had been wrapping up the installation of the glasstop computer system when he arrived. The techs left quickly when he walked in, and there were still some boxes and packing material strewn about.

He had just finished a phone call with Dean Arnall, where he had praised the craftsman's workmanship and thanked him for finishing the desk so quickly. Arnall had deflected the thanks to the shipping company, who had apparently driven all night from D.C. to Missouri to load the desk, and then had it at the White House by 10 p.m. the next evening.

Martin was now preparing for a press conference that would take place this afternoon at the White House. He imagined what the reaction would be if he addressed the Majestic issue out-of-the-blue at a routine press conference. It would be an absolute circus, he thought. Of course, a weekly White House briefing was not the correct venue to make this announcement. He would need to address the nation in a primetime telecast. But not before briefing the rest of his cabinet and hundreds of government leaders.

Based on the reaction he received from Alan Kingman that morning, he assumed it would be very difficult to keep the story quiet once he briefed the larger audience. The leaks to the media would start immediately. Once that occurred, global panic would not be far behind. The reaction from other nations, both ally and enemy, was a major concern as well.

ANTHONY WILSON

Martin still had a hard time accepting the fact that this crisis was almost 90 years old and only a small group of Americans knew about it. Based on the evidence taken from the crash site, the aliens planned to set-up habitats near geographic high-points all over the globe. It might be understandable that Truman wanted to keep the initial investigation internal. But once the global threat was uncovered, leadership should have sought a global solution. It was counter to Martin's style to second-guess his predecessors, but this was the wrong decision; one that he needed to correct, despite the painful consequences.

Martin leaned back and surveyed the room which now reflected all of the changes he had requested. The artwork that adorned the Oval Office walls looked even more impressive against the fresh paint. Martin's eye caught the small brass plate above the closet door. He tapped the calendar icon on his glasstop. He still had ten minutes until his next appointment, a Green Room meet-and-greet with the Super Bowl champions.

Martin walked across the office and slowly opened the closet door. It looked the same. He pushed his way past the flags to the back of the closet. As before, just past the last flag was the living room. As he entered, he noticed that the room seemed brighter. He looked up expecting the see an overhead light, then realized that the walls had been painted. Still light brown, but less dusty. The trappings of the room were still blended together, but each item was a bit more detailed. He noticed several ceramic birds on the fireplace mantle. They had been there before, but appeared more cluttered. The puppercat was lying in front of the fireplace, staring at Martin through those blue eyes. It shifted its gaze as the log in the fireplace slipped backward. Martin glanced at the glowing brown embers that sparked underneath the log, and then noticed Mortimer, who was leaning the fireplace poker against the hearth.

Flame from the growing fire reflected in Mortimer's eyes as he turned toward his guest. "Well hello, Mr. President. It's been a while."

Though he did not remember doing so, Martin had moved to the center of the room. "Yes, it has. How long would you say?"

"That's hard to tell," said Mortimer. "Time is often difficult to define."

"I'm still not sure what to think of all this," said the President.

"This?"

"You. This room." Martin said, looking around. "Why are you here?"

"To help you, Mr. President,"

"You've said that before, but why me? Do you help others?"

"I have helped, and will help, anyone who asks me."

Martin shifted uneasily. "But if I'm the only one who can see you, how do you help others?"

Mortimer smiled calmly. "Seeing me is less important than what you see in yourself."

"Which is a good thing, 'cuz you're not much to look at Mort!" Martin turned around to find Emma seated behind him. The puppercat was in her lap. Emma snorted, obviously amused with herself.

Mortimer sighed and looked upward as if seeking some sort of divine intervention. "Great glory be, Emma. You promised you would stay out of this for a bit."

The puppercat looked up at Emma, anticipating a reply.

"Well excuse me for not knowing how long a *bit* is," said Emma. "Besides, he likes me too. Ain't that right Jimmy?"

"Emma!" said Mortimer sternly, with a heavy step forward. The puppercat shot under the table. "You will address our guest with respect."

"How was that not respectful? That's his name isn't it," Emma looked at the President. "Isn't it?"

Martin started to answer, but Mortimer spoke first. "Nevermind her, Mr. President, and please accept my apology. Where were we before we were interrupted?"

"I...I don't remember," said Martin, heading quickly toward the wall. "I need to get back to work."

"Wait," said Emma eagerly. "Please stay for coffee."

"I don't have time," said Martin, darting behind the tapestry. "I'm sorry."

He continued quickly past the flags. Reaching for the closet door was the last thing he remembered before everything went dark. Just as he lost consciousness, he felt a searing pain in his head, and he heard the fireplace crackle one last time.

CHAPTER 19

Tuesday, February 24, 2037
The White House

M r. President. Mr. President…Sir…"
James Patrick Martin attempted to open his eyes. The left one flickered, but the right one would not cooperate. He blinked, waited a few seconds, and opened the left eye again. With one eye his vision was fuzzy, but he was able to recognize Gwen. She was face-to-face with him. Townsend was leaning over her shoulder with a concerned look on his face.

"Are you still with us?" asked Gwen. She readjusted the towel she was holding against the right side of his head. That explained why he could not open his right eye.

Martin took a couple of deep breaths and nodded. He realized he was sitting in a chair against the wall. The closet door stood open a few feet away from him. He could see spots of blood on the towel. "What happened?"

"You smacked yourself a good one, Mr. President," said Townsend, looking less stressed. "You sure did."

Martin reached toward his aching head.

"Just sit here," said Gwen, gentling grabbing his hand. "The medics are on the way."

"How long was I out?" asked Martin.

"Not more than a minute," said Gwen. "Townsend caught you before you hit the floor."

"Yes, sir," said Townsend. He was smiling now. "I was cleaning up the mess the computer guys left. I didn't think you were in here. Then I heard a rumble from the closet. I was heading over here as you came out. You hit your head on the side of that closet, something awful."

"I heard it all the way in my office," added Gwen. "So did the Secret Service guys. They nearly trampled me running in here."

"They may have beat her in here," laughed Townsend. "But she shooed 'em away mighty fast."

Aside from the throbbing in his head, Martin was starting to feel better. "Well, I'm sorry for creating all this excitement, but thanks for the help."

A few seconds later two Marine corpsmen arrived. They were escorted into the room by Chris Boone, who then stood stoically at the door talking into the cuff of his shirt.

The medics carefully helped Martin walk to the couch so he could recline while they assessed his injuries. One corpsman attached a wire to the President's PIB and began recording his vitals. The other medic shone a penlight into Martin's eyes. After an interminable amount of poking, prodding and penlight waving, it was announced that, aside from a nasty bump on the head, the President was fine.

"Good," said Martin. "I've got a football team to congratulate."

The medic looked bewildered. "Ah, well, Mr. President, you are going to need a couple of stitches to close that wound. We'll need to transport you to Bethesda for that."

Hearing the medic's statement, Chris Boone immediately returned to his shirt cuff to request that Marine One be brought to the South Lawn.

"Stand down Agent Boone. I'm not going to Bethesda." said Martin, turning back to the medic. "You can do it here."

Now even more nervous, the medic cleared his throat, "Sir, we really should have a plastic surgeon do this."

"Are you telling me you've never stitched a wound?" asked Martin.

"No. We've stitched plenty of wounds," said the medic. "But it will look much nicer if the plastic surgeon does it."

The President could not believe what he was hearing. "Give me a mirror, please."

Gwen slipped away and was back in an instant with a hand mirror. She held it in front of the President's face. He moved his head slightly down and forward to get a good view. The cut was deep, but small, and right along his hairline.

"Sew it up here," said Martin. "If you get in trouble, I'll issue a presidential pardon."

CHAPTER 20

Tuesday, February 24, 2037
The White House

Rae Martin carefully pressed a fresh ice compress onto her husband's head.

"Looks like the swelling has gone down a little," she said. "It really doesn't look that bad."

James was lying in bed with his head propped up against several pillows. He held the TV remote and was flipping from channel-to-channel. The flat screen was mounted on the wall on the far side of the room. He stopped on a news report. He was standing in front of several large football players. A white bandage was prominent on the right side of his forehead. The text at the bottom of the screen read, "Atlanta Falcons Visit White House." Martin was holding a Falcons' jersey.

"Despite the fact that it was at the hands of my beloved Chiefs, I congratulate you on your Super Bowl win," Martin said on the video. "I toyed with the idea of wearing a Kansas City jersey to this meeting, but decided I'd suffered enough abuse for one day."

Several of the Falcons laughed as the reporter's voice cut in.

"The ceremony was delayed for almost an hour because President Martin reportedly suffered a nasty fall in the Oval Office."

James switched to another channel which was showing part of the White House press briefing from the afternoon. He was in the middle of answering a correspondent's question. "My turn was a little too wide, and I hit the side of the closet door."

"Why were you in the closet?" asked another member of the press.

"That's classified," said the President sternly. Then he smiled. "I was inspecting the beautiful redecorating job that was just completed in the Oval Office. I believe we have pictures of the office and the new desk available for all of you."

James continued to flip through the channels. The late-night comedians were having a field day at his expense.

"Martin is the first President to come out of the closet while in office…"

Martin clicked the remote again.

"President Martin reportedly just finished the Bill Clinton autobiography entitled *Interns in the Closet.*"

James hit the power button and looked at Rae who was holding back a laugh.

"Why were you in the closet?" asked Rae. "Did they really redecorate the closet?"

"No," he answered. "But I wouldn't have known that if I hadn't checked."

He removed the ice pack, placed it on the nightstand, and clicked off the lights. After rearranging his pillows, he leaned across the bed and kissed Rae lightly on the cheek.

"There weren't any interns in the closet," he said in his most disappointed voice.

Rae turned over and smacked him with her pillow.

CHAPTER 21

Tuesday, February 24, 2037
Washington, D.C.

Across the city, Rudolph Overton was sitting up in bed. He too was watching the news reports of President Martin's eventful day. He was up later than usual. Despite two consecutive long days, Overton was energized. His plan was coming together, his patience paying off.

He watched intently as one of the networks cycled through several pictures of the newly decorated Oval Office. The new paint scheme gave the office a more intellectual look. The new desk was impressive. Overton tried to recall how many different decors he had seen in that office through the years. *They do seem to recycle and repeat*, he thought.

Overton had been in the Oval Office a few times during his career. Various presidents had sought his advice on matters of foreign trade. He had served on several presidential councils and commissions.

It had been many years, perhaps more than a decade, since he had last visited the White House. He doubted President Rosemont even knew who he was. That was fine with him. Rosemont was worthless, even more worthless than the countless drones that had preceded him.

The jury was still out on the new guy. Not that he would prove to be a better man than those who had served before. But, unlike his predecessors, President Martin would be forced to take action, to be held accountable. Rudolph was looking forward to this. He planned to have a front-row seat.

CHAPTER 22

Wednesday, February 25, 2037
The White House

A warm light from somewhere above mixed with a chilly wind as James Martin walked slowly through the Rose Garden.

It seemed too early in the season for rosebuds, but they were all around him. The buds, and the leaves, and the grass, and the trees were caramel-colored, like cream swirling in coffee.

In the distance there were soft voices, almost whispers. The words were familiar, but they were carried away on the gentle wind before they could be fully understood.

Two men stood down the path; one short, one tall. They were sharing a secret. Martin moved to join them as a gust of wind rustled the leaves. The bushes grew thicker, blocking the path. The wind blew harder, and a single rosebud began to glow and swirl. He reached out as the bud began to open. The glow grew stronger as the brown petals parted and twisted into the face of...Emma.

"Hello, James. Out for a stroll?

"James? James!"

Martin woke with a jolt. Rae was looking down at him, her hand on his chest. "James. Sweetheart. Are you alright?" she asked.

He shifted and reached for the bandage on his head.

"Does your head hurt?" she asked.

"No," said James. "I think I was dreaming."

Rae rubbed his arm. "You kept saying Kennedy."

"Yeah, he was there."

"JFK?" asked Rae.

"Yeah, weird."

"Do you want to talk about it?" she asked.

James thought for a moment. "No. But I want to tell you about something else."

CHAPTER 23

Wednesday, February 25, 2037
The White House

The President and first lady sat in the residence dining room drinking coffee. Both were unable to sleep after their early morning talk.

James fixated on his cup as he contemplated his dream. He didn't usually have such vivid dreams, and he rarely remembered them the next day. Last night's dream was crystal clear. He now realized the voices he heard were Mortimer and John F. Kennedy. He didn't know what they were talking about, but it seemed oddly familiar to his closet conversations.

He knew his visits to the closet also had to be some type of dream. But he could not explain the eagle token that he carried in his pocket, or the stitches in his head. Both were very real.

As difficult as it was for James to come to grips with his current thoughts, it was doubly difficult for Rae. She had listened intently as her husband sat beside her in bed, talking about crashed UFOs, alien autopsies, and magical sheets of grey metal that tracked an asteroid loaded with giant poisonous respirators. At first, she thought his head injury was more serious, and then she thought he was still dreaming. But as he spoke in more detail about General Bolser, Alan Kingman, and the staff at the Pentagon, Rae realized her husband was totally coherent and absolutely serious. She also knew that, while fun-loving and humorous, James Martin would never take a joke this far, especially when it involved the office that he held.

"What are you going to do about it?" asked Rae.

James snapped out of his trance. "I don't know the specifics yet. But people have the right to know about this. Maybe that asteroid will fly right past us and nothing will happen. But if the end of the world is coming in a matter of months, it shouldn't sneak up on people."

Rae nodded. "What can I do?"

"I don't know that either," he said. "But I'm certain you can be a lot of help. You have experience with this sort of thing–disasters and crises."

She thought for a moment. "I know how to piece things together after they're torn apart. I know how to prepare for disasters. But this is very different. You can run from a tornado or a hurricane. People can move out of a war zone. But there's nowhere to run in this scenario."

James looked back at his coffee cup. The swirls were gone. "Let's get you to the Pentagon so you can see some of this for yourself. Once you have some perspective, maybe some ideas will come."

CHAPTER 24

Wednesday, February 25, 2037
The White House

Alan Kingman was pacing back-and-forth behind the sofa in the Oval Office. "I agree with you. It's the right thing to do. But this will cause absolute chaos the likes of which we've never seen."

President Martin was seated in a chair across from the sofa. He had just told his Chief of Staff that his decision was final. He was going public with the story–full disclosure. Kingman was in problem-solving mode, which always required him to be standing and usually moving.

"Have you thought about timing?" asked Kingman.

"A little," said Martin. "The next United Nations session is in April. It's our turn to set that agenda. We should go public just prior to that and use the U.N. forum to deal with the fallout."

"That gives us a little more than a month," said Kingman. "We'll have to be careful how we stage the internal communication."

"I'd like to pull in some members of the senior staff to get input on messaging," said Martin.

Kingman nodded. "Maybe they will have some ideas on how to keep the leaks from happening."

"We won't be able to prevent the leaks," said Martin.

Kingman stopped pacing. "Why not? Make it clear that their job is on the line if they talk."

"Think about it, Alan. How much weight would the threat of losing a job carry when faced with the threat of alien invasion just six months from now?"

The pacing resumed. "You're right. So how do we stop the leaks?"

"I don't think we need to," said Martin. "Who would believe it?

"Good point. I barely believe it myself, and I've seen all the evidence."

Martin stood and walked to his desk. "I think that evidence is the key to our messaging."

"How's that?" asked Kingman.

"Everything that we've seen from the Majestic team adds credibility to the threat. But the evidence also gives us hope."

"Hope?" said Kingman.

"Yes. It's clear that the Hecatians *intended* to inhabit Earth. But there is no evidence that they still have the capability to do it. In fact, the disappearing planet in the Canis Major galaxy may have been their planet. That asteroid may be carrying an advanced scout team that is now stranded, with no place to go."

Kingman stopped pacing and thought for a moment. "Dr. Lakey did say that the number of craft on the asteroid has not changed since it returned to our solar system in 2000."

"And Dr. Lindsey's simulator shows most of the craft are only capable of carrying up to three passengers," said Martin.

"Still, with their advanced technology, they might be capable of taking over Earth and making it habitable with just a few beings," said Kingman.

"True. But our message has to have some element of hope, and this is our best, or only, hope."

"What about the other countries. There focus will be on why we've hidden this for the better part of a century."

"Those will be difficult conversations which must be handled with extreme sensitivity," said Martin. "Fortunately, I've got just the right person for the job."

CHAPTER 25

Wednesday, February 25, 2037
The State Department

J ordyn Turner sat at her desk in the State Department. Nearing the end of the first full month in her new position, Turner had sat in this office on exactly three occasions. With little exception, the rest of her time had been spent on a plane, or on the ground in another country.

She had just received a call summoning her to the White House for a late afternoon meeting with the President. At least this trip would not require crossing time zones.

As Secretary of State, Turner represented the United States around the globe. She spoke for the President. She influenced policy. She kept the most demanding schedule of anyone on the planet. And, she loved every minute of it.

James Patrick Martin had officially nominated Turner to be Secretary of State two days after the election. But he had told Turner she was his pick back in July, on the same day that he informed her that she would not be his running mate.

"Jordyn, you are by far the most qualified person to be Vice President," Martin had told her. "But you are the only person I trust to be Secretary of State."

While she had hoped for the VP spot, Turner quickly warmed to the idea and the challenge of being Secretary of State. She was confident that her background in Congress had prepared her for this key position. She had spent over a decade in Washington, first as a Representative and then as a Senator from her home state of North Carolina.

Turner had a long history with President Martin. They had first met as teenagers when they attended the same prep school in western North Carolina. Turner had enrolled prior to her freshman year in high school. Martin arrived one year later. They became friendly rivals toward the end of their junior year, when they ran against each other for Student Body President. Turner won the election by three votes, a fact relished by the media during her confirmation period.

After earning a law degree from UNC, Turner began her career as a corporate attorney with a firm based in Raleigh. She was on the fast-track to partner when she realized that she was more interested in the direction of the country than the direction of companies she represented. She accepted a position as council to North Carolina's senior Senator. This move provided her with the political connections she needed to eventually garner support for her congressional run.

Martin and Turner reconnected when both arrived at the Capitol, Turner as a newly-elected Representative from North Carolina, and Martin as the junior Senator from Missouri. Both were considered up-and-comers within the Independent Action Party.

In her first year in office, Turner was assigned to the House Committee on Foreign Affairs. Later, as a Senator, she served on the Senate Foreign Relations Committee. Her work-ethic and collaborative track-record made her a good fit for the Secretary of State. She sailed through her confirmation hearings with little resistance.

Thus began her whirlwind travel schedule. As Secretary, Turner handled most of the foreign affairs during the early part of the Martin administration while President Martin focused primarily on domestic matters. While she was adjusting to her new role, Turner wondered why Martin was so internally-focused.

She was about to find out.

CHAPTER 26

Wednesday, February 25, 2037
The White House

W e had no right to withhold this type of information from the rest of world," said Jordyn Turner, near the end of her hour-long meeting with President Martin and Alan Kingman.

Martin and Kingman had used the need to brief the Secretary of State as an opportunity to practice portions of their presentation for the rest of the staff that would take place next week.

"Agreed," said both men, in unison.

Turner reached for the grey sheet with the jagged tear that the President had commandeered from General Bolser. She studied it again, but found no more answers than she had the first two times she picked it up.

"What were they thinking?" asked Turner. "Did they think the issue would just go away?"

"I think Truman wanted to thoroughly study things before he did anything," said Kingman. "But I think the rest of them just kicked the can down the road, assuming someone else would figure it out."

Martin nodded in agreement. "Some could argue that Kennedy took action. Using the space race with the Russians to cloak our efforts to place deep-space telescopes on the moon was pretty slick."

"But isn't that really just another lie?" asked Turner. "Shouldn't a space-monitoring initiative be a global effort?"

"In the 1960s, only the U.S. and the Soviet Union had any type of space program," said Kingman. "And we weren't getting along too well at the time."

"True," said Turner. "But if the rest of the world had known what we were truly working on, perhaps other countries would have invested in space exploration too. Maybe those oil-rich countries in the Middle-East would have invested in finding a solution to this problem instead of battling over their borders."

President Martin ran his fingers through his hair, careful not to rip off his bandage. "You're dead on Jordyn. There are a lot of things that could have, and should have, been done differently. But we've got to get to work to correct the damage."

"Please tell me this includes informing the rest of the planet of this threat," said Turner.

"That's why you're here," said Martin. "Alan and I will be briefing the rest of the staff next week. Then we will get to work on how to best present this to the general public. In the meantime, you need to put together a plan to inform key leaders in other countries. You will handle our major allies and our sensitive relationships. Use diplomats and ambassadors for other countries."

Turner nodded. "What's the timing on this?"

"The U.N. is in session in April," said Kingman. "The President will address the public the night before. We will need to have briefed other governments in advance of that speech."

"But not too far in advance," added Martin. "We know there will be leaks and rumors, but we should try to control it as much as possible."

Turner stood and shook hands with both Kingman and Martin. "I'll put a plan together."

"One more thing," said the President. "I've arranged for you and the first lady to go to the Pentagon tomorrow morning. The Majestic staff will run you through the same presentations that they showed us. I think you'll find it helpful."

CHAPTER 27

Thursday, February 26, 2037
The White House

James and Rae Martin relaxed in the living room of the White House residence having spent the earlier part of the evening hosting a state dinner.

"Do me a favor sweetheart," said Rae.

"Anything, my love."

"The next time you send me to the Pentagon to have the life scared out of me, try to time it so I don't have to spend the same night playing smiling hostess to hundreds of people."

James cringed and reached for Rae's feet, thinking a foot massage might get him out of the dog house. "I didn't think of that. Sorry."

"Jordyn Turner would like to strangle you as well. At least she was able to slip away from the dinner early."

"I take it you found Majestic as enlightening as I did?"

"That's one way to describe it. A better word might be terrifying."

James thought back on his visit to Majestic. "I agree. It is disturbing."

"You're not really considering making that video available to the public, are you?"

James nodded. "I think the public deserves full disclosure."

Rae considered her words carefully, and then decided to take the direct approach. "You can't do that, James. Showing that video would be like showing victims of a plane crash. It's too much. Can't you at least cut out the gory parts?"

"Maybe, as long as we can still convey the danger."

Rae leaned deeper into the sofa, enjoying the foot rub. "In all my life, I would never have dreamed I would see what I saw today. The spacecraft, and the alien bodies."

James flashed back to his last encounter with Mortimer and Emma.

"I know what you mean," said James. "And not just the aliens, it's kind of creepy around here, too."

Rae opened her eyes. "You mean here in the White House?"

"Yes," said James.

"Are you seeing people in the bathroom again?"

James laughed. "No. I'm talking about the West Wing."

Rae raised herself and slipped a pillow behind her back. "What are you seeing?"

"Nothing specific," said James. "Just shadows and odd sounds."

"You said you were dreaming about President Kennedy the other night. Is that what you're talking about?"

James nodded. "Yes, that and a few other things."

"You do know that the White House is haunted don't you?" asked Rae.

James rolled his eyes. "Do you really believe that stuff?"

"Hey, after this morning, I don't know what I believe anymore, but just about every President who has ever lived here has reported strange happenings. Lincoln's ghost is the most popular, but there have been lots of other spirits documented. Aaron Ash told me there is a cat that haunts the basement. It apparently changes form the closer you get to it."

James stopped rubbing his wife's feet. "A cat?"

"Don't stop," said Rae, pushing a foot back into James' hands. "Mr. Ash said it was called Demon Cat. Apparently it shows up just before a major disaster or national crisis. President Kennedy supposedly saw it just before he was assassinated."

"I never knew you were such an expert on the paranormal," said James. "I should hire you as my spiritual advisor."

Rae slipped back down into the sofa. "You don't have to hire me. Rub my feet, and I'll advise you on any subject you choose. Free of charge."

CHAPTER 28

Tuesday, March 3, 2037
The White House

Thus far, this had been the quietest meeting of his presidency. The Cabinet Room was filled to capacity. In addition to the cabinet members, the deputies and assistants were present. In short, anyone with an office in the West Wing was in the room.

After announcing that the agenda for the meeting was "eyes and ears only," meaning no handwritten or recorded notes, and no discussion outside of the room, the President and Chief of Staff methodically spelled out the alien situation. They started with the New Mexico crash site, progressed to the Majestic project objectives, and ended with the August invasion and habitation scenario.

The only visual aid for the meeting was the grey metallic sheet, with the jagged tear and purple writing, which was passed around the room. The intent was to summarize the facts into a 50-minute oral presentation, then send groups of staff members to the Pentagon over the next few days to view the rest of the evidence for themselves.

"All we can hope to do today is get their attention and make sure they understand the gravity of the situation," Martin had said to Kingman prior to the meeting.

Based on the stunned silence, and the wide eyes, it appeared they had met their objective.

"Each of you was selected for a position in this administration based on your proven ability to respond to the issues of the day," said the President in closing. "Now I know that none of us could have dreamed of a situation as bizarre as this, and it's natural to initially react with fear and trepidation. I understand that each of you will need some time to process this, along with what you will see at the Pentagon. But I need you to quickly get to work on helping us figure out how we are going to tell the rest of country, and the rest of the world."

Martin paused to let his words sink in. Every eye in the room was on him. "Are there any questions?"

General Knudsen cleared his throat. "Have you determined what action we will take against the Hecatians?"

"We have determined that there is no viable action that we can take against the Hecatians," said the President.

"Blow up the asteroid," said Knudsen.

Kingman's neck turned red as he peered at Knudsen. "General, we've discussed this…"

The President raised his hand, cutting off Kingman mid-sentence. "Let's take this off-line."

Martin surveyed the room for a few more seconds. With the exception of Kingman, who was still glaring at Knudsen, most of the audience was now avoiding eye contact.

"Thank you everyone. We will talk again soon," said Martin, motioning the General toward the Oval Office.

Martin intercepted Kingman as he worked his way toward the exit. "I'll take care of Knudsen. You take a walk and cool off."

"He was totally out of line," said Kingman, looking for somewhere to pace.

"I'll take care of it," said Martin.

A minute later the President entered the Oval Office and closed the door behind him. General Knudsen was looking out the window and picking at his fingernails.

"What was that about?" asked Martin, his irritation evident.

Knudsen turned to face the President. "We need to defend this planet."

"We don't have the technology to do what you're suggesting, General. I thought General Bolser made that abundantly clear.

What's more, I believe I made it abundantly clear that we were not going to pursue a military option."

Knudsen's reddening face matched his hair color. "You can't make this go away with a bunch of speeches and prayers."

"You may very well be right. But it's my decision, and I've made it. You either get onboard, or get out."

CHAPTER 29

Monday, March 9, 2037
The White House

President Martin tapped his PIB and fingered through to his daily calendar. As was the case on most days, his schedule was packed with back-to-back, seven-minute phone calls, or face-to-face sessions, sandwiched between longer formal meetings. Most of the seven-minute meetings had a second meeting scheduled for the same time.

Gwen Hardin orchestrated this fluid calendar by telling the person, or persons, meeting with the President that they had precisely *three* minutes to conduct their business. Ultimately, the President would decide if the discussion warranted the full seven minutes. If the President stood, or tapped his pen repeatedly on his desk, Gwen would politely interrupt the meeting by announcing the next call or guest.

The seven-minute time slots were key because, in theory, they gave the President one minute every quarter-hour to himself. It was a chance to take a breath, have a snack, compose a thought, or stretch his legs. In reality, and despite Gwen's best efforts, the 60-second respite rarely materialized.

Today the President was, surprisingly, on schedule. He had left a financial briefing five minutes early to ensure he was on-time for his next face-to-face. Most meetings were subject to the President's schedule, but Martin made an effort not to keep certain people waiting. This was out of respect for the person's position, not necessarily the person.

"President Rosemont. Nice to see you," Martin said as he whisked into the Oval Office. "I hope you haven't been waiting long."

"Not at all," said the former President. "I was just admiring what you've done with the place."

Martin motioned toward the chairs in the center of the room. "I appreciate you stopping by."

Rosemont sat. "You want to give me back this job?"

Martin laughed. "Well, I have to admit there are days I might consider that, if it were an option."

"Thankfully, it's not an option. I still feel bad about sticking you with this mess. I truly am sorry."

"I know you are. But you were just the last in a long line."

Rosemont thought for a moment. "What's your plan?"

"We're going public, a few weeks from now, just before the U.N. session. We're in the process of briefing the staff. Kingman and the VP are making the rounds in Congress. Jordyn Turner and her staff are gearing up for foreign meetings."

"What's the message?

"We're going to tell whole story. The Majestic staff is preparing a series of public demonstrations."

Rosemont nervously picked at his suit coat, "You know this will set off a worldwide panic."

"Yes, it likely will," said Martin. "But we think we can offer some hopeful scenarios. What's your view on the planet that disappeared from the Canis Major galaxy at the turn of the century?"

"I've always been hopeful that it was Hecate, the alien's home planet," said Rosemont.

"Exactly. If it was, they may not be capable of carrying out their plan anymore."

"But what if they *are* still capable? Have you considered military options?"

Martin let out an exasperated laugh. "Unless you forgot to tell me about an ultra-classified asteroid pulverizer, I don't think we have a military option."

Rosemont smiled in an attempt to hide his embarrassment. "I assume Knudsen's resignation had something to do with this?"

"Yes it did. My plan is to reinstate General Bolser right after we go public with the alien story. In the meantime, he's agreed to fill the spot on an interim basis."

"That makes sense," said Rosemont. "He understands this mess better than anyone."

"He's been a big help."

"I wish I could be more help to you, James. We're in the process of moving to our home in the Keys. But you know the Secret Service can always track me down if you need me."

Martin nodded and checked his watch. Rosemont understood the signal that the meeting was over. Both men stood and walked toward the door.

"One more question, on a different subject," said Martin as he stopped and motioned toward the far wall. "Why did you have the fireplace removed?"

Rosemont seemed surprised by the question. "It just never felt like it belonged in here. It distracted me."

CHAPTER 30

Monday, March 9, 2037
The White House

Gwen Hardin tapped lightly on the door and stepped into the Oval Office. "Do you need anything else before I leave for the evening, Mr. President?"

Martin checked the clock on his desk. 7:02 p.m. "What are you still doing here? You know we can't afford to pay you overtime."

"It's good that you still have your sense of humor," said Gwen, sounding more like a concerned mother than an efficient secretary. "How are you holding up?"

The President leaned back in his chair and put both hands behind his head. "I'm alright. One of the benefits of being President is that I get to surround myself with incredibly smart and hardworking people. That certainly makes this job easier."

Gwen took another step into the room. "I was in the group that went to the Pentagon today."

Martin stood and leaned against the corner of his desk. "What did you think?"

"It was unnerving, especially the video."

"Yes, it was."

Gwen thought for moment. "What do you think is going to happen in August?"

Rae had asked him that same question after she returned from the Pentagon. "My gut tells me that we are going to be fine."

Gwen brightened a bit. "That's good. Your gut has a pretty good track record."

Martin laughed and headed back around his desk. "My gut also tells me that I need to head upstairs for dinner."

"Good night, Mr. President."

"Drive safe, Gwen."

He shuffled through some of the papers on his desk, and then tapped his PIB to check his schedule for the morning. His mind returned to Gwen's last question. He had been truthful with Rae and Gwen. Deep down he did believe that everything was going to be fine.

He eyed the brass plate above the closet door across the room.

So why worry billions of people by making this public?

How could he be so sure that he needed to disclose this issue to the world, yet at the same time, feel confident that the danger would pass?

He stared at the non-existent fireplace across the room. Rosemont was distracted by it. But he was drawn to it.

Martin walked across the office and slowly opened the closet door. Quickly, but carefully, he slipped past the flag stands and emerged from behind the tapestry.

The fireplace was roaring and illuminating the room in a sandy brown glow that was much brighter than previous visits. The puppercat was stretched across one of the chairs in the middle of the room, eyeing Martin as he moved toward the fireplace.

The mantle was covered with several ceramic birds. The one in the middle looked much like one of the birds his grandfather had. Martin reached to examine it, but it was stuck to the mantle.

"Glue."

Martin spun around to find Emma sitting in the chair that was previously occupied by the puppercat, which was now lying in the other chair.

"Pardon?" said Martin.

"Glue," repeated Emma, pointing at the mantle with her nose. "Keeps the kids from knocking them over. Those things are breakable."

"Yes, I suppose they are," said Martin, glancing back at the bird. "Is that an eagle?"

"Actually, it's a hawk," said Mortimer, who was now seated opposite Emma. The puppercat was now napping in Emma's lap. "It's a common misidentification. Both are classified as raptors. Eagles are usually larger, but they look very much the same in flight."

"Blah, blah, blah," interrupted Emma. "Here we go with the bird lessons again. You think you're so smart."

Mortimer took a deep breath and turned toward Emma. She met his gaze with a blink. "Do you mind letting me answer our guest's question?"

"He just asked if it was an eagle," said Emma. "Just tell him it's a hawk. Or let him think it's an eagle. It's just a bird. Who cares?"

Mortimer stared at Emma.

"Fine," said Emma. "Finish your lecture."

Mortimer turned back to the President. "As I was saying, they look much alike. The real difference is in their symbolic meaning. Eagles symbolize power. Hawks symbolize acute perception and quick discernment."

Martin fished the coin from his pocket. "Is this a hawk or an eagle?"

Without looking at the coin, Mortimer smiled. "It is a hawk, Mr. President. Perception and discernment are often much more valuable than power."

"But what if the perception is wrong?" asked Martin.

"That's where discernment comes in," answered Mortimer.

Martin thought for a moment.

The fireplace crackled.

"I don't think he gets it," said Emma.

"Emma, please," Mortimer pleaded.

"Maybe if you took him out in the garden like you did that nice Kennedy fellow," said Emma.

Mortimer raised a hand. "You're not helping."

"Did you know President Kennedy?" asked Martin.

"Yes," said Mortimer. "We visited together."

"Now *he* was a real looker," said Emma. "But those kids of his, they were always running around and being rowdy."

Mortimer cleared his throat.

Emma leaned forward and whispered to Martin. "They were the reason I glued the birds down."

"So he visited you in this room, just like I visit you?" asked Martin.

"Your visits are similar, but not exactly the same," said Mortimer. "And, yes, we talked here, and in the garden."

"Did you ever talk with President Kennedy in the basement?" asked Martin.

Mortimer thought. "Not that I recall. Why do you ask?"

"Ever hear of Demon Cat?" asked Martin, glancing at the puppercat who quickly awoke and glared back at the President.

Emma let out a snort and covered the puppercat's ears. "We don't like to use that word."

Mortimer looked slightly ashamed. "Yes, well, I'm afraid this one does have a tendency to roam around a bit."

Martin ran his fingers through his hair and looked toward the tapestry. "I think I'd better be going."

"Come back anytime," said Mortimer.

"Anytime," repeated Emma.

As Martin pulled back the tapestry, the puppercat darted down between the empty chairs and stretched out in front of the fire.

The President moved past the flags, keeping his forehead a safe distance from the doorjamb. He closed the closet door behind him just as Townsend entered the room.

"Good evening, Mr. President," said Townsend. "I thought you had gone to the residence."

"I was just finishing up," said Martin, glancing at the closet door.

Townsend hesitated, "Sir, are you looking for something? Maybe I can find it for you."

"No, I…I just find the closet peaceful sometimes," said Martin. "It gives me a place to focus my thoughts."

"You don't have to explain anything to me, sir," said Townsend. "If you don't mind me saying, I sometimes found your grandfather crawling out from under his desk. He had the exact same look on this face that you do when you come out of the closet."

Martin smirked. "What was he doing under the desk?"

"Well, that's the funny thing," said Townsend. "He would say he was adjusting the phone cords. But he would never let me get the phone guys in here to check on things."

Martin thought for a moment. "I guess maybe this odd behavior runs in the family."

"I don't think it's a family thing, sir. It more likely goes with the position. In the years after the 9/11 attacks, the man in charge would sit on that sofa and talk to his dog for hours."

President Martin laughed. "So you're saying you have to be a little crazy to occupy this office?"

"No, Mr. President. I'm just saying that you've got a stressful job," said Townsend. "If you want to steal a moment in the closet from time-to-time, you go ahead and do it."

CHAPTER 31

Monday, April 6, 2037
The White House

It was possible that this was the best roast beef he had ever tasted. It was a shame he couldn't eat more than two bites.

"I'm sure they can wrap that up for later," said Rae, reaching across the table for her husband's hand.

James nodded and squeezed her fingers. It was just over an hour until he would address the nation, and the rest of the world. Just over an hour until he sent a chill of fear through every man, woman and child on the planet.

He was absolutely certain that he was doing the right thing. He was equally certain that he was going to be sick. Throughout his career, he had addressed hundreds of thousands of people in person, and millions more through the media. But tonight, he was having a serious bout of stage fright.

There could be no more delay. The opening session of the U.N. was two days away. The entire United States government–both houses of Congress, the entire cabinet, the White House staff, and the governor of every state in the Union–had been briefed. Secretary of State Turner and her staff of ambassadors and emissaries had informed the leaders of every country on the planet. The resulting leaks and speculation had worked the global media into a frenzy.

Over the last three weeks, an endless string of rumors had circumnavigated the planet. The most common theme was pending terrorist attacks against world capitals. Several religions groups sited evidence of the second-coming and/or Armageddon. The most creative story involved invasion by a group of aliens that had been hiding on the dark side of the moon for decades.

James pushed his dinner plate to the side and grabbed the printout of his speech.

"Which draft is that?" asked Rae.

"I lost count a few days ago. But this is final, unless I make a change on the fly. It's already on the teleprompter."

The speechwriters had revised and rewritten the address over and over again. Knowing the magnitude of the speech, everyone wanted to ensure that they added their special touch for the sake of posterity. Or more likely, for the sake of being listed as a contributor in the history books.

While the writers had tweaked the individual words, the tone of the speech came from the President with input from Secretary Turner. Rae had also made several good suggestions.

"It's a good speech, James. Stop obsessing."

He nodded, still reading the last page. "I don't know. Maybe I should throw in some French."

Rae almost choked on her last drink of wine. "That should be fun."

One of the many things that James found charming about his wife was the fact that she was fluent in French. Ever the romantic, he surprised his new bride on their wedding day by memorizing a line in French.

During the couple's first dance as husband and wife, James whispered in Rae's ear *"Je vous aime avec toute ma poitrine."* Rae had been unable to speak during the rest of the song because she was laughing so hard. After she had regained her composure, she translated for the groom, "You love me with all your chest."

It was the last time that James Martin had tried to speak French.

"On second thought, maybe not," he said.

He closed the folder, stood, and walked to the opposite end of the table where three neckties were neatly folded. His black suit coat was hanging over an empty chair. "Speaking of obsessing, have you decided which tie I should wear?"

His public relations staff had recommended bringing in a professional stylist to handle the wardrobe decisions for the speech. James had rejected that idea immediately, noting that he could dress himself. Later he decided that a little help from Rae couldn't hurt.

"I have, indeed, made my decision," said Rae, "none of them."

James raised an eyebrow.

Rae produced a box that had been sitting in her lap during dinner. "Here you go."

"Did you make me a tie?" James joked.

"No, I did not make you a tie. Just open it."

He removed the lid and pulled out a deep purple silk tie with a subtle silver and navy diagonal stripe. It was the tie he had worn on his wedding day.

"Now, this is perfect. Why didn't I think of this?"

Rae placed the tie around his neck and started working the knot. "The last time you wore this ended up being a pretty good day. I figured it might still have some magic in it."

Glossy-eyed, James kissed his wife. "Do you remember when I told you that the only way my lofty career plans would work out was if you were by my side?"

"Yes," said Rae.

"This is what I was talking about."

Rae reached up and flipped the hair on his forehead. "You're sweet."

James turned his head to the side. "Do you think my manly gnarled scar will distract people tonight?"

Rae rolled her eyes. "Your hair covers what little scar there is."

James stuck out his lower lip.

"I'm sorry," said Rae. "Yes, your manly gnarled gash will make all the women swoon and all the men jealous."

James smiled. "That's more like it."

CHAPTER 32

President Martin was seated behind his desk in the Oval Office. There was a single camera positioned in front of the desk with a clear glass pane in front of the lens. Martin could see the first few lines of his speech when he looked directly into the camera.

"Three minutes, Mr. President."

Two stands, each supporting very bright lights, flanked the camera. The technicians were making final adjustments to ensure the President's face was properly lit, without casting a harsh glare on the teleprompter.

From the back of the room, another technician asked Martin to say a few words as a sound check.

Martin thought for a moment. "Perception and discernment are often much more valuable than power."

Skyboards around the globe were displaying the presidential seal along with the headline "President James P. Martin Address." A countdown clock, showing just over a minute, appeared below the seal.

"One minute, Mr. President. Let's clear out." Typically, the room was filled with bystanders whenever the President addressed the nation from the Oval Office. Tonight, Martin had asked that only essential staff remain in the room. He did not want to risk distraction or have the temptation to look at someone for help. When the door to the office closed, only the President, the sound tech and the cameraman remained.

"Five," said the cameraman, holding up five fingers. He lowered one finger at a time, and then pointed at the President.

"Good Evening. Tonight, I'm addressing you from the Oval Office in the West Wing of the White House in Washington, D.C. My comments are being broadcast across the United States, and around the world.

"I come to you to tell you about an event that happened in the United States almost 90 years ago. This event has the potential to impact our planet in the immediate future.

"In the summer of 1947, an aircraft of unknown origin crashed near Roswell, New Mexico, in the southwestern part of the United States. In the days that followed, a number of theories emerged about the crash. Some reported it was a weather balloon, and others speculated that it was a secret and advanced military aircraft.

"In fact, the object that crashed was an alien spacecraft."

The cameraman and sound tech exchanged shocked glances as the President paused briefly.

"Under the direction of then-President Harry Truman, United States Air Force personnel collected debris from the crash site and took it to Roswell Army Air Field for analysis. Some years later, the crash site debris was transferred to a different site that had been built specifically to further enhance the study. This project was given the codename Majestic and has been in operation ever since.

"In the coming days, staff from the Majestic project will provide exhibits of the alien craft. Those presentations will be broadcast globally."

Martin held the grey metal sheet with the jagged tear in front of him. "This is a piece that was recovered from the crash site." He crushed the sheet into a ball and held it in front of the camera as it unfolded back to its original shape. "Decades of study by the Majestic team have determined that the craft is of advanced design and made from materials that are unknown to our planet."

He then held the sheet upright so the camera could move in closer. The cryptic symbols glowed purple. "There is also evidence of an advanced intelligence with communication and propulsion capabilities that far exceed our knowledge."

The President paused briefly as the camera refocused on him. "In addition to the debris from the craft, three alien bodies were recovered from the crash site. These remains were also initially examined at Roswell Army Air Field and subsequently transferred to the Majestic site. The presentations by the Majestic staff in the coming days will also include detailed information about the alien remains.

"While much about the alien physiology and technology remains unknown, the Majestic project has been successful in determining the likely location of these aliens' home planet. There is a galaxy called Canis Major that exists not far from the outer edges of our Milky Way. There is a solar system on the edge of Canis Major that is about 25,000 light years from our sun. The Majestic team has evidence that indicates these aliens were from a planet, which early Majestic team members named Hecate, in that solar system. The evidence also suggests that the alien's home planet, Hecate, was destroyed around the turn of this century.

"The Majestic team has also determined that an unknown number of aliens, or Hecatians, escaped their planet in spacecraft similar to the one that crashed in New Mexico. They currently inhabit an asteroid that is traveling through our solar system. This asteroid, known as 29075 DA, will pass within 100,000 miles of the Earth in August of this year.

"While there is evidence that the original intent of this alien race was to inhabit our planet, we now believe the surviving number of Hecatians is not sufficient to carry out their initial plan.

"Again, in the coming days, staff from the Majestic project will share evidence in support of these assessments.

"We believe the threat to our planet is low, but we recognize that our understanding of the intelligence and capabilities of this alien race is unknown. This is why we are disclosing this information to the rest of the planet.

"I understand and support my predecessors' decisions to gain a thorough understanding of the initial crash, as well as the intentions of the Hecatians. However, it is also my belief that once this threat was discovered, it was the responsibility of the United States to notify the rest of humanity. Beginning with tonight's address, I pledge to rectify this oversight.

"As part of the upcoming United Nations session, we will work with representatives from other countries around the globe to fully understand the level of threat against our planet, and to determine the most appropriate actions to take to protect ourselves.

"I want to reiterate that the members of the Majestic project, some of whom have dedicated their entire careers to studying this situation, are fully convinced that we are not in danger.

"One of the United States' most beloved and respected leaders, Franklin Delano Roosevelt, once said 'the only thing we have to fear is fear itself.' We must resist the urge to turn this surprising and uncomfortable revelation into an unnecessary crisis.

"In closing, let me quote another of humanities' great leaders, Winston Churchill. 'Come then, let us go forward together with our united strength.'

"Thank you, and good night."

CHAPTER 33

Monday, April 6, 2037
Washington, D.C.

Rudolph Overton pointed the remote at the far wall of his study and clicked the television off. He was seated at his desk; tears filled his eyes as he fingered the three items from the box in front of him.

So many years he had waited for this moment. Finally, he had heard a confession from an American President. It was bittersweet. He would now have to give up one of his most prized possessions.

He reached for the phone, dialed a number from memory, and waited for an answer.

"We need to meet," said Overton. "I have something for you. It's time to carry out our plan."

CHAPTER 34

Three days later, President Martin sat in his assigned seat at the U.N. General Assembly. Throughout the day, he had endured the wrath of a parade of nations whose representatives took turns lashing out at the United States for decades of deceit.

The preceding day had featured presentations from key members of the Majestic team. Emily Lindsey had addressed the assembly in person, with members of her team providing backup via video from the Pentagon. Lindsey walked the group through the major pieces recovered from the crash site. She also used the simulator to give everyone a view of the intact spacecraft.

Lindsey was followed by Dennis Gordon, who facilitated a review of the smaller artifacts. Several of the respiratory units and grey screens were passed through the group at the U.N. The Pentagon video link was used to display the alien bodies as Gordon explained the little that was known about the Hecatian physiology. He ended with an introduction of the Roswell autopsy video that had been edited for public viewing. All video showing President Truman had been removed, as had the more graphic footage of the medical team's demise. Still, even with the toned-down content, the U.N. members viewing the video were audibly and physically upset by what they saw.

The mood worsened in the afternoon when Kyle Lakey took to the podium to provide details about the asteroid and the Canis Major solar system. Despite Lakey's best effort to explain how the alien's home planet had most likely been destroyed, most in the audience honed-in on the alien's plan to inhabit Earth. The demonstration using the grey sheet, with the holographic model of the planet showing the details of the large mountain-top respirators planted to convert the Earth's atmosphere, elicited the same type of outburst as the Roswell video did earlier in the day.

All of the presentations had been recorded and immediately broadcast around the world. Every major newspaper on the planet ran one of three pictures on the front page: the alien bodies, the holographic purple Earth with the mountain-top Hecatian Death Machines, or a Majestic technician holding the car-sized piece of spacecraft over her head.

Public response mirrored that of the U.N. audience. General panic and unrest ensued. Media outlets scrambled to find experts on alien technology and invasion theory. Websites with references to Canis Major, 29075 DA, Majestic, and any form of Hecate crashed because of heavy traffic. The town of Little Mountain, S.C., population 3,000, was overrun with tourists simply because its zip code, 29075, matched the asteroid's name.

President Martin's proactive move to close the major stock markets in the days following his announcement had proved worthwhile. Major banks around the world had also agreed to reduce hours and withdrawal limits, thanks to the efforts of Secretary of State Turner.

Currently, Feng Li Bo, the Premier of the People's Republic of China was at the podium. His demeanor was less agitated than previous speakers, but his message was stern and clear. Martin listened to his comments through headphones which were connected to an interpreter who was translating the speaker's comments from Mandarin Chinese to English.

"The purpose of the United Nations is to bring all nations of the world together to work for peace, based on the principles of justice, human dignity and the well-being of all people. Not just the well-being of the citizens of the United States."

Martin resisted the urge to wipe his brow. He realized a television camera had been permanently aimed at him all day in an effort to catch his reactions to the scathing comments. The Chinese representative was paraphrasing the official mission statement of the United Nations. Martin had planned to do the same when he addressed the assembly later in the day. He calmly opened his portfolio and scribbled some notes in the margin of his speech, while making sure that he still appeared to be listening intently to the speaker.

"Chinese history on this planet dates back 3,500 years. We will not stand idly by and allow our very existence to be threatened, be that by an enemy from this planet, or any other."

A few hours later President Martin stood before the United Nations audience. As host nation, the United States had the honor of giving the final address.

As further protest, representatives from a handful of countries, including China, had exited the room as Martin took the stage. Still, the venue was tightly packed, including hundreds of media personnel.

"Ladies and gentlemen of the Assembly," began Martin. "I have spent the last several hours listening intently as many of you addressed this body. Two distinct themes have been common in your messages. First, you are disappointed in the way that the United States has handled this situation in the past. You feel that a potential threat of this magnitude should have been shared globally, and much earlier. I share your disappointment. Every member of my administration shares your disappointment.

"Second, you view this threat as daunting, and you are unsure how to respond to protect the citizens of your countries. I share your uncertainty with how to respond to this daunting threat.

"I do, however, recognize that there are some certainties within this situation. It is a certainty that this is a global threat. And it is a certainty that we must develop a global response. Just as it was inappropriate for the United States to isolate its efforts to understand the threat, it is inappropriate for any country to isolate itself in determining an appropriate response.

"Some of you have suggested a military action. The best defense is a strong offense. Historically, that strategy has often proven to be true. But history has never faced this type of threat. We have no weapons that can match this technology. We are not capable of the level of space travel that would be required to reach the asteroid. Further, our most credible evidence indicates a strong likelihood that the Hecatians are no longer able to carry out their initial plan. As Dr. Lakey explained earlier, there are less than three dozen spacecraft on that asteroid. That means there are no more than 100 alien beings. Clearly, they would not need to invade this entire planet and establish a livable atmosphere for 100 beings. We must resist the urge to overreact to this threat from a position of fear.

"Earlier today, Premier Feng, from the People's Republic of China, quoted from this body's mission statement. He reminded us of our commitment to work together for the well-being of all people. The second part of that mission statement states that the United Nations gives us the opportunity to balance global interdependence and national interest when addressing international problems.

"Yes, the United States did not afford the rest of the world the opportunity to work together over the past nine decades. As I have said, I regret that fact. But I cannot change that fact. What is more important is that we are here, now. We are here, today. Ready to share everything we have learned; ready to work together, with the brightest minds on this planet, for the well-being of this planet.

"Every member of the Majestic team that you met today, and every member of their staff, is available to partner with you to explore meaningful solutions to this threat. Please join this effort."

As Martin walked from the podium, polite applause echoed through the room. It was not an enthusiastic response, but was not complete rejection, either.

Chris Boone met Martin as he left the stage. "Mr. President, please come with me." As they walked down a hallway, an unusually large number of Secret Service agents surrounded the pair.

Boone led the President into a back room where General Bolser was waiting, with even more security.

"Come on, General," said Martin. "I know I'm not the most popular guy in the building, but aren't we overreacting a little bit here?"

"No, sir," said Bolser. "There has been a separate incident."

"What?" asked Martin.

The General locked eyes with the President. "President Rosemont has been killed."

CHAPTER 35

Rae Martin was sitting on a couch in the White House residence reading an e-book on her PIB. She was trying to occupy her mind while she waited for her husband to return from New York.

Earlier in the evening, Alan Kingman had stopped by, with a regimen of secret service agents, to tell her about President Rosemont. She had reluctantly agreed to remain in the residence until further notice.

There was a rap on the door, followed by two secret service agents entering the room. President Martin quickly followed. "I see you're under arrest, too," he said, motioning the agents out of the room and closing the door.

Rae greeted him with a short kiss, and a long hug.

"What have they told you?" asked James.

"Just that Rosemont was found shot to death in the library of his home in the Keys. Alan said they are stepping-up security around all of the former Presidents."

James led Rae back toward the couch. "Yeah, it was quite the spectacle around Air Force One at JFK."

"Do they think you are in danger?"

"No more than usual. But there was some evidence found near Rosemont that has everyone on edge."

"What was that?" asked Rae.

"They haven't announced this to the media, but General Bolser says they found an alien artifact near Rosemont."

Rae tried to process the comment. "What kind of artifact?"

"They are shipping it to the Majestic team for verification, but it appears to be the missing section of the grey sheet with the jagged tear."

"Maybe Rosemont had kept it as a souvenir," speculated Rae.

James shook his head. "Nope, that piece has been missing since day one. This is either a fake, or Majestic has not been as top secret as we thought."

"How did it go at the U.N.? I saw your speech on TV, but it was hard to gauge the reaction."

"The reaction was pretty middle-of-the-road from most countries. I talked with Jordyn Turner on the flight home. Her biggest concern is China going rogue with some kind of crazy reaction."

"Like what?"

"They've had some success with space launches recently. They are gearing-up for an unmanned mission to Mars in the next 18 months. It's possible they might try to go after the asteroid with some type of warhead on a spacedrone. Our intelligence thinks it would be a longshot for them to get anywhere near the asteroid."

"How about I change the subject to something that might be more realistic," said Rae, as she reactivated her PIB and fingered through to a document. "I had a call with some old friends from the Red Cross this afternoon. They had an interesting idea."

James craned his neck to get a better view of the document. "Let's hear it."

"In the broadcast presentations, the Majestic staff said they have had some success protecting researchers from the alien respiratory toxins with the use of certain types of gas-masks."

"That's right," said James. "The charcoal-based respirators seem to dissipate the alien toxin."

"The Red Cross wants to manufacture gas-masks for everyone on the planet."

"There has been no large-scale testing," he said. "There's no proof these masks would provide adequate protection."

"True, but it's a place to start," said Rae. "It would give people hope, and the sense that we are taking action to try to protect everyone."

James nodded. "It would be quite a project to manufacture eight billion masks, let alone distribute them."

Rae laughed. "I think that's why they called me. My husband has lots of connections."

CHAPTER 36

"Thanks, General. I'll get back to you later this morning."
President Martin hung up the phone and turned his attention to
Alan Kingman, who had been waiting patiently in front of the desk
in the Oval Office.

"Bolser said the Majestic staff is certain that the strip of metal
found next to Rosemont's body is the missing piece from the original alien grey sheet," said Martin. "It's the same unknown metal. It
also has some of the same glowing purple symbols."

Kingman scratched the top of his head and started pacing.
"Rosemont was shot through the heart, at close range, in the study at
his home. And, by the way, the killer just happens to be in possession of a century-old piece of metal from another planet. What the
hell?"

"I got nothing," said the President.

"How could anyone have gotten past his secret service detail?"
asked Kingman.

"Apparently there were a lot of people in the house," said Martin. "There were six men from the moving company who were un-
loading furniture. They had been screened, but pretty much had the
run of the place."

"I can't believe I'm saying this, but could it have been the
Hecatians?" asked Kingman, still pacing.

"That's the thought that kept me up last night," said the President. "It's crazy to even think it. But then all of this is crazy."

"Someone would have seen the spacecraft," said Kingman.

"What if there wasn't a spacecraft?" asked Martin.

Kingman stopped pacing and sat down on the sofa. "What are you saying? An alien was posing as a furniture mover, or maybe a secret service agent?"

"I don't know, maybe," said the President. "Maybe there was a fourth Hecatian on that crashed spacecraft. Maybe there have been other spacecraft that came here, undetected, and dropped off other aliens. Maybe they can assume human form. All we really know for sure is they appear to be indestructible. We don't know what else they are capable of."

"Are you trying to tell me that you're an alien, Mr. President?" Kingman said, trying to keep a straight face.

Martin laughed. "Yak, I can always count on you for a moment of levity."

"It's a gift," said Kingman.

A tone sounded from the President's desk, followed by Gwen Hardin's voice. "Mr. President, I have Secretary Turner on the line for you."

"Thank you, Gwen," said Martin as he tapped the speaker icon on his glasstop. "Hello Jordyn, I've got Alan Kingman here with me."

"Mr. President, Mr. Kingman, good morning," said Turner.

"I've lost track of where you are," said Martin. "But I'm guessing it's not morning there."

"Correct. I'm in Abu Dhabi. It's approaching 7 p.m. here."

"Do you ever sleep?" asked Kingman.

Turner sighed. "Some. My plane's not as nice as the President's, but it's not bad. My biggest problem is the phone."

"A lot of that is my doing," said Martin. "Every leader on the planet wants to talk with me. I've routed most of them through your office."

"As you should," said Turner. "We are keeping up with it. So far everyone wants to either officially express their displeasure with the US, or they want to offer to help in any way they can."

"Has anyone offered up any real ideas?" asked Martin.

"A few, I've connected them with the appropriate Majestic staff."

"Good," said Martin. "Anything new from China?"

"Not directly, but North Korea told our ambassador that they support China's plan for a military offensive. So there may be something to that armed spacedrone rumor."

CHAPTER 37

Monday, April 13, 2037
The White House

Three days later, and thirty minutes late, President Martin hurried into the Roosevelt Room in the White House. The Majestic core team, General Bolser, Emily Lindsey, Kyle Lakey, and Dennis Gordon had been there for half an hour ready to brief the President.

"I'm sorry for the delay," said Martin. "I know you all are as stretched as I am. I would have preferred to come to the Pentagon for this meeting and save all of you the trip. But the Secret Service is making me stick close to home whenever possible."

"We understand, Mr. President," said General Bolser. "We appreciate you sending the helicopter for us. Traffic is a challenge today."

Martin was well-aware of the traffic issues. President Rosemont's funeral had snarled the streets in downtown D.C. Even the President's motorcade was delayed while returning to the White House.

"Let's start with anything new," said Martin.

Kyle Lakey tapped a few buttons on the conference room table, and then walked toward a projection screen on the far wall. "Members of Japan's Aerospace Exploration Program contacted us through Secretary of State Turner with a suggestion that we think is worth considering."

A flat map of the earth filled the screen. Lakey used a laser-pointer as he talked. "We all recall the Hecatian's model of our planet with respirator symbols placed on mountain tops. We assume their model was based on the need to create a habitable environment for a large part of their population. The Japan team agrees with our assessment that the Hecatian's home planet is gone. They also agree that the aliens on the asteroid are most likely all that survived. Therefore, they no longer need to convert the entire planet to their environment.

"The Japanese suggest that we identify areas of low population on Earth that would be suitable for the aliens to create a habitat. We could then offer the aliens those locations as an alternative to their original plan."

"Interesting," said the President. "But it's going to be difficult to find those locations."

Lakey clicked to another map. "Maybe not, the vast majority of the Earth's population has settled near water, because water is the source of life for all humans. But that's not necessarily the case for the Hecatians. There is no evidence of water on the asteroid. If it was Hecate that blew up, it would have heated to the point that water would have been gone long before the explosion."

"So, if they don't need water, they could conceivably survive in the desert," said Martin.

"Deserts, grasslands, woodlands," said Lakey. "But they would need elevated areas nearby to place their respirators."

"How many low population areas on Earth fit that bill," asked Martin.

Lakey clicked his laser pointer again. "There are a few suitable locations. This map shows some of the better options. Ayers Rock is a large sandstone formation in central Australia. It's surrounded by desert, with little population."

After clicking to a map of the United States and Canada, Lakey pointed to a section of southern Canada. "The Cypress Hills in southwestern Saskatchewan and southeastern Alberta. And there is a region in northern Montana that has three mile-high peaks within a 25-mile radius, Gold Butte, West Butte and Mt. Brown."

Lakey clicked back to a global map. "There are similar locations in Brazil and on the African continent."

"This idea has merit, Dr. Lakey," said the President. "Get me some solid population numbers for these sites. I'll take it from there."

Martin looked around the room, "Dr. Lindsey, what do you have?"

"Apparently, we are not the only country who has been quiet about encounters with alien spacecraft," said Lindsey. "We've had calls from England, Germany and Mexico–all of them have debris from crash sites that they want us to look at. We haven't got our hands on anything yet, but based on photos and video review, most of the material appears to have originated on Earth; weather drones, satellites, that kind of thing."

General Bolser straightened in his chair. "We would not expect to find another craft similar to the Roswell crash. If there were another alien craft on the planet, we think it would display on the alien's tracking map, similar to the crashed craft that is being housed at the Pentagon."

Everyone in the room nodded in agreement.

"Anything else?" said Martin, motioning toward Lindsey.

"We are still getting several requests for special presentations of the Majestic items," said Lindsey. "We are sticking with the requirement for other countries to send delegates to us. We don't want to take this show on the road. So far, only Japan has come to visit. We expect more in the coming weeks."

"Good, thank you," said Martin. "Dr. Gordon, I understand you've been working with the first lady."

"That's right, Mr. President," said Gordon. "We provided Mrs. Martin and her Red Cross colleagues with the specifics on the respiratory devices that have provided the best protection to our staff. We also discussed the manufacturers that would be best suited to mass produce such a large volume."

"Where are those manufacturers located?" asked Martin.

"England, Germany and the U.S. have the largest producers, but just about every industrialized country on the planet has at least one manufacturer," said Gordon. "We are putting together production specs that can be shared with all of the manufacturers."

"What's the likelihood that they can produce eight billion plus masks in just a couple of months?" asked Martin.

Gordon smiled. "Better than we initially assumed. Most of the world's militaries already outfit their troops with masks that are similar to what we would be producing. We also catch a break in that the most effective masks are charcoal-based. These are the easiest to produce."

"That's good, now we just need to figure out how to get these masks into the hands of every human being on the planet." The President paused and looked around the room. "Any ideas?"

Silence.

CHAPTER 38

President Martin motioned toward Gwen Hardin as he walked into the Oval Office.

"I need you to set up another call with Secretary Turner as soon as she is available. I also need to speak with the Governor of Montana. And try to find me an expert on global shipping."

Gwen scribbled a few lines into a notebook then squinted at the President. "Global shipping?"

"Yes. Someone who would know how to get a package to everyone on the planet very quickly."

Gwen thought for a moment. "Like Santa Claus?"

"Exactly!" exclaimed Martin. "Get me Santa on the phone. Better yet, bring him to this office."

"I'll see what I can do," said Gwen.

Martin sat at his desk and started reading through his notes from the meeting with the Majestic staff. It was encouraging that Japan had come forward with a viable option for action. He hoped he could get good cooperation from Montana's state legislature and the Canadian government. He tapped his PIB and fingered over to his atlas app, and after a few clicks he was looking at a map of northern Montana and southern Canada. Based on the amount of white space, there were not a lot of people on that part of the continent. He would get pushback, but he already knew that any offering of land to the aliens would have to include the United States.

China was a growing concern. After the Majestic meeting, General Bolser had pulled Martin to the side and told him of a military build-up around China's two primary space exploration facilities.

Bolser also reported increased activity near one of China's nuclear armament storage locations.

As if that weren't enough, General Knudsen was spending a lot of time with the media promoting his views on appropriate military options.

Gwen interrupted his thoughts. "Mr. President, the first lady is here to see you."

Martin clicked off his PIB and rose to meet his wife. After one look at Rae, he knew something was wrong. He could see that she had been crying.

"Is it dad?" asked Martin.

Rae hugged him and pulled him tight, she was crying again. "No sweetheart... It's your mom... She's gone."

CHAPTER 39

Monday, April 13, 2037
40,000 ft. above West Virginia

A few hours later, the President and first lady sat together in the private sleeping quarters on Air Force One. They were avoiding another confrontation with the Secret Service. Chris Boone had adamantly objected to the announcement that the President would be staying at his parent's home in Joplin, Missouri. "We just lost a President," Boone had said. "I can't allow you to go into an unsecure location."

James had walked away, red-faced, without saying a word.

Rae was equally perturbed, but not as quiet. "Agent Boone, I, more than anyone, appreciate what you do for my husband every day," she had passed by Boone without making eye-contact. "But the man just lost his mother. We are staying with his father. Figure it out."

After a few minutes of solitude on the plane, a call came in through James' PIB. He tapped the speakerphone icon.

"Hello, Deanna," said James.

"Hi, Jimmy. Can you talk?" his sister asked.

"Yes, we're in the air now," he said. "Rae is here with me. Do you know any more?"

Deanna sighed. "Not much. It was a heart attack for sure. They think it happened late last night. But since she didn't have a history of heart problems, they are going to do an autopsy to find out what caused it."

"She was supposed to be the healthy one, Sis," said James. His voice was starting to crack.

"I know," said Deanna. "I was with her yesterday. She was just fine."

"How's dad taking this?" asked James.

"I'm with him now. I don't think he understands what's going on. He just keeps asking 'Where's Bet?' over and over."

James shook his head. Tears filled his eyes again. "I never thought…"

Rae switched to a seat beside her husband and put an arm around him. "We should be there in a couple of hours, Deanna. James and I will help make the arrangements."

"Where will the two of you be staying?"

"We'll be right there with dad," said Rae.

"He'll like that, Rae. That's good to hear," said Deanna. "How did you get the Secret Service to sign-off on that?"

James and Rae both let out a laugh.

"We'll tell you about that when we get there," said Rae.

"Ok. I'll have the coffee waiting," said Deanna. "Love you both."

James tapped off his PIB and looked at Rae, still teary-eyed. "I can't believe this is happening."

Rae nodded. She held back her own tears, trying to be the strong one. "It will be OK, sweetheart. We'll get through it."

CHAPTER 40

Tuesday, April 14, 2037
Washington, D.C.

Just before dawn, Rudolph Overton sat in an oversized leather chair in his study, reading a newspaper and sipping tea.

He had learned of the President's personal loss the day before. The morning papers had provided a little more detail, including the fact that the President was now in Missouri.

So much for one man to deal with all at once, thought Overton, as he poured more tea from a ceramic pot. *This is better than I could ever have imagined.*

Overton had yet to come down from the tremendous high generated by the death of President Rosemont. While there had been no mention of the artifact found with Rosemont in any of the media reports, there had been plenty of speculation that his murder was connected to the alien story.

And now the sitting President was rushing off to deal with a personal matter. This would have to impact the man's ability to focus. Overton knew that he could not have orchestrated this better himself.

Perhaps the Gods are finally with me, he thought. *Fate has recognized the worthiness of vengeance and decided to switch sides.*

CHAPTER 41

Thursday, April 16, 2037
Joplin, Missouri

James Martin gazed out the living room window of his sister's house as he enjoyed his fourth chocolate-chip cookie. Deanna and her husband, Paul, had lived in this house for almost twenty years. But, to James, it still felt like his grandparent's house.

James remembered looking out the same window on the day that they buried his grandfather, and years later after his grandmother's funeral. It was always the same. The house was quiet, and the media and well-wishers were restricted to the sidewalk and street in front of the house.

The President knew that the Secret Service cringed every time he got near a window. Still, they preferred that he be at this house, which was more secluded and more easily secured than his parent's house. He and Rae had spent three uneventful nights with his father. It was obvious that his dad missed his mother, but James did not think his dad fully grasped that his wife was dead.

Deanna entered the room with another plate of cookies.

"No way, Sis," said James. "You've got to cut me off."

Deanna feigned disappointment. "OK, I'll just send them out to those nice Secret Service agents."

"No, no. Wrap them up and we'll take them with us. I'm sure Rae will eat a few more on the flight home."

Deanna smiled and sat the plate on the coffee table. She wrapped her arms around her brother and took in a big breath. "It was a nice service. Mom would have been pleased."

"It was. I wish dad would have at least tried to attend," said James. "Please thank Paul again for staying with him during the service."

"He was honored to do that," said Deanna. "Those two still get along pretty well. Paul always heads right over there if dad needs something fixed."

James smiled as he looked around the room. "Speaking of fixing things, you two sure have kept this house looking good." He spotted a ceramic bird over the fireplace mantle. "Is that one of Papa's birds?"

Deanna nodded. "Yes. He had so many of them we can't possibly display them all. There's a bunch at the library, several here, and a few at dad's house."

James sat down on the sofa and grabbed a pillow. "Do you remember when I busted that bird after Papa's funeral?"

"I sure do," Deanna said, her eyes widening. "That was his first bird, probably his favorite."

"It was an eagle, right?"

"No," answered Deanna. She moved down the hallway toward a closet. "It's a hawk. In fact, grandpa used to love to talk about the difference between the two, something about the hawk being smarter."

James felt a chill run down his spine.

After a minute, Deanna returned to the living room carrying a cardboard box. "Here's the victim."

"You kept the broken bird," said James, moving to the edge of the sofa. "All these years?"

"Come on, Jimmy," laughed Deanna. "You know you can't throw away anything that belonged to a President."

James carefully removed some of the broken pieces. It was definitely a hawk. He could tell by the shape of the beak.

"Who gave this to Papa?" he asked.

"That's a big mystery. He got it very early in his presidency, maybe even the first day. But there's no record of who gave it to him. It sat behind his desk in the Oval Office for eight years."

James examined the base of the statue. His heart skipped a beat when he read what was etched on the bottom... *Down Under 2:05 p.m.*

He thought for a moment. "Sis, where's grandpa's presidential desk now?"

"It's back on display at the library," said Deanna. "Why?"

James placed the ceramic pieces back in the box and stood up. "We need to go to the library. Now."

CHAPTER 42

Thursday, April 16, 2037
Joplin, Missouri

Deanna Faye pulled her SUV next to the back entrance of the James Warren Patrick Presidential Library. President Martin and Chris Boone were riding in the back seat. Martin was wearing a Kansas City Royals baseball hat and sunglasses.

Martin had convinced Agent Boone to approve the unscheduled trip by limiting his options.

"You can go with us, or we will go alone," the President had told the agent.

Since the President was most often seen riding in a big black behemoth of a limousine, Deanna's white SUV with the tinted windows provided a perfect diversion. Just a few of the media hounds stalking Deanna's house noticed when she pulled out of the garage and no one followed her.

The library was closed for the day to allow the staff to attend Betty Martin's funeral. Deanna unlocked the back door. The President asked Boone to stand guard at the door, promising he would only be inside for a few minutes.

James and Deanna walked down a dimly lit hallway toward the Oval Office display.

"Sis, would you mind giving me a moment in private?" asked James.

"Absolutely," said Deanna. "I need to pick up a couple things from my office."

As his sister walked toward the opposite end of the library, James stepped inside the velvet rope that separate the office display from the main walkway. He surveyed the full scale model of the

Oval Office which was complete with every detail, except for the hidden closets.

James walked around his grandfather's desk. It had survived its trip to D.C. and back unscathed. He sat in the chair and swiveled to face the credenza that sat behind the desk. A replica of the shattered hawk figurine sat next to a picture of his grandmother. He checked the bottom of the statues' base. Nothing.

He thought back to what he had seen on the broken base at Deanna's house earlier that morning. *Down Under 2:05 p.m.* He knew what the numbers represented. What did *Down Under* mean?

He turned back to the desk and fingered the buttons on the phone. It was just like he remembered, except the buttons did not light-up and flash. What had Townsend said about his grandfather's obsession with the phone lines under the desk?

James knelt down on both knees and looked under the desk. There were no phone lines. He was about to sit back in the chair when he noticed a notch toward the bottom of the display board that covered the kneehole at the front of the desk. He crawled further under the desk and pulled at the notch, nothing. Then he lifted the notch upward. To his surprise, the board rose and curled back into the underside of the desktop, like a little garage door.

James stared, wide-eyed and mouth agape at what was behind the sliding panel…a staircase. He leaned in closer and saw about a dozen steps leading down into a dimly lit room.

Crackle.

James rubbed his eyes. *Impossible*, he thought.

After a moment, he swung his legs around and carefully descended the stairs. The lighting improved with each step. Just as he reached the bottom of the staircase, something raced across his path and into the adjoining room. James peered around the corner and found the puppercat sitting in an armchair.

Martin was standing in the familiar sand-colored living room. The fireplace glowed with the same eerie brown light. The only difference was his location in the room. The tapestries were on the far wall rather than behind him. He looked back again at the stairway. He had not noticed it on previous visits.

"Hello, Mr. President. I'm glad to see you again." Mortimer was sitting in the chair previously occupied by the puppercat. Emma was seated next to him.

The President again glanced back at the stairway, trying to make some sense of the odd circumstance. Then he realized that accessing the room from a closet in the Oval Office was no less odd than the stairs.

"You knew my grandfather," said Martin. The words came out as a cross between a statement and a question.

Mortimer's eyes brightened. "Indeed. He was a magnificent man. You remind me of him."

Emma listened to Mortimer intently, nodding as he spoke. Then she turned back to Martin, blinking in anticipation.

"Did he visit you often?" asked Martin.

Mortimer nodded. "Several times, yes. Whenever he had a particular need."

Martin looked confused.

Mortimer continued. "Your grandfather faced similar challenges to yours. He would drop by with questions, especially when things were a bit…overwhelming."

Martin ran his fingers through his hair. "Overwhelming, I know that feeling, especially the last few days."

Mortimer smiled sympathetically. "You have certainly had a lot on your mind lately. I'm very sorry about your mother, James."

Emma nodded again, then shot Mortimer a look. "Now hold on just a gosh-darn minute! How come you can call him James, but you get all worked-up when I do it?"

Mortimer closed his eyes and inhaled deeply. "Emma, there is a time and a place for everything. You should consider that. Often, the best response is silent reflection."

"You didn't answer my question, you old coot," said Emma with one defiant blink.

"I will discuss this with you later, Emma" said Mortimer. "Now, if you don't mind, let's see if our guest has other questions."

Emma shrugged and snorted. She turned back to Martin and blinked a couple of times. "Well?"

Martin raised his eyebrows and then turned his attention back to Mortimer. "How did my grandfather deal with the overwhelming times?"

"Your grandfather was a master at organizing his thoughts and prioritizing his focus," said Mortimer. "He had confidence in his decisions. Once he made a decision, he refused to let unrelated distractions affect his resolve."

Martin thought for a moment. "That's easier said than done. But it makes perfect sense."

"It does take practice," Mortimer said with a grin. "Your grandfather constantly worked at it. So did President Kennedy. Lincoln, too."

"Lincoln?" said Martin, bringing back the confused look.

"Abe," said Emma. "Tall guy, big black hat…"

"Emma!" scolded Mortimer.

Martin shifted his stance and glanced again at the stairway. "So you have offered your, uh…help to other Presidents? Not just the ones dealing with the aliens?"

"Certainly," said Mortimer. "Presidents have dealt with other challenges, not just those from far away galaxies."

"And you've met with all of them?" asked Martin.

"Only the ones who sought me out," said Mortimer. "Most, but not all."

Martin nodded his head slowly. "All the way back to Washington?"

"Oh yes, General Washington was here all the time," said Mortimer.

Emma brightened. "George had a devil of a time deciding if he would take on a second term. He changed his mind at the last moment. I think it was something he saw in his coffee swirls."

Both Martin and Mortimer stared at Emma.

"What?" said Emma. "OK, sorry. *President Washington* had a devil of a…"

"Thank you, Emma," said Mortimer with a raised hand. "We understand."

Emma leaned back in her chair, seemingly pleased with herself.

"So you've been here for 250 some odd years?" asked Martin.

"As I've said before, time is often difficult to define," said Mortimer.

Martin glanced at the staircase. "I suppose space is difficult to define as well?"

Mortimer's eyes twinkled in the firelight. "Equally difficult. But time and space are not important. It's what a man finds in his heart that is important."

Martin stepped back toward the stairs. "I should be going. Thank you."

"It is always my pleasure," said Mortimer, as Martin climbed upward.

When he reached the top of the stairs, James gingerly crawled from under the desk and reached back to lower the desk panel. He was careful not to bang his head as he rose from the floor.

After a moment, he walked to the opposite end of the library and tapped on his sister's office door.

Deanna jumped with surprise. "Oh goodness, Jimmy, you scared me. That didn't take long."

"Sorry, Sis," said James, checking his watch. "You're right, it didn't take long at all."

"Did you find what you were looking for?" asked Deanna.

James smiled. "Yes, I did. Thank you."

CHAPTER 43

Tuesday, April 21, 2037
Washington, D.C.

President Martin climbed into his limousine after a meeting with key legislators at the Capitol Building. Alan Kingman was waiting for him with a fresh copy of the Washington Post.

"Brace yourself," said Kingman. "This is not good."

The headline on the front page read, HECATIAN HOMICIDE? A picture of the alien artifact, lying on a blood-stained carpet, appeared under the headline. The caption noted that the item had been found next to the former President's dead body.

"How did they get this?" asked Martin as he skimmed the related story.

Kingman shook his head. "We don't know. The White House Press Office got a call from the New York Times about an hour ago asking for a comment. Apparently, every major newspaper, broadcast network and website has it. This was the first paper to hit the streets."

"We must have a mole. The Secret Service and the Majestic team are the only people who knew about this."

"Do you think the picture is legit?" Kingman activated his PIB and fingered through various websites.

"It matches what Bolser showed me. But I don't think it really matters if the photo is real or not. The story is accurate."

"Some of the major websites already have it posted." Kingman continued his scan of cyberspace. "The media is going to go crazy over this. It's the first new stuff they've had since the Majestic presentations."

Martin nodded in agreement.

"How do we spin it?" asked Kingman.

"How about, we don't spin it. Let's just tell them the truth."

Kingman thought for a moment and then clicked his phone icon. "OK. I'll arrange a press conference."

"Don't bother." The President hit a button on the door panel and the tinted privacy window behind the limo driver lowered. "Change in destination."

A few minutes later, the President's limo pulled directly in front of the Capitol Building. The rest of the motorcade surrounded the limo. The President and Chief of Staff remained in the back seat. Agent Boone, who had been riding next to the driver, turned to address the President. He was trying desperately to hide his angst.

"Mr. President, we can't possibly protect you out in the open like this."

"How about if I stay in the limo?" asked Martin.

Boone was not expecting that answer, neither was Kingman. After a few seconds of uncomfortable silence, Kingman asked, "What good will sitting in front of the Capitol do, Mr. President?"

Martin pointed to the Capitol stairs. No less than a dozen people were running down the stairs, most carrying television cameras. They were the young newbie newshounds assigned to camp-out at the Capitol waiting for a congressional bigwig to walk outside. Legislators had used this group to orchestrate impromptu press conferences for decades.

"Well, I'll be damned," said Kingman.

Boone jumped out of the limo and organized his crew in a semicircle around the back of the limo. Reporters jockeyed for position, set-up their cameras, and speculated among themselves as to who was in the limo.

After a few minutes, the President lowered his window.

"Good afternoon," said Martin. "I would like to address the various news reports regarding the alien artifact that was found near President Rosemont."

The reporters all stood in stunned silence.

"The reports are true. A piece of metal, matching the jagged edge from the grey sheet found at the original Roswell crash site, was found by Secret Service agents when President Rosemont's body was discovered. The piece was delivered to the Majestic team for authentication. That team believes the artifact is real. The decision was made to withhold this information from the public because it was a key piece of evidence in an ongoing homicide investigation. This was in keeping with long-established standards for crimes of this type. The Majestic team, and all members of my administration, will have no further comment on this subject. Thank you for your time."

Before anyone had a chance to fully process what he had said, the President raised the window and turned back to his wide-eyed Chief of Staff. "How was that?"

CHAPTER 44

Saturday, April 25, 2037
The White House

James Martin walked slowly across the Rose Garden lawn toward the West Wing. He was dressed in khakis and a blue oxford shirt; no tie, no suit coat. Working on the weekend was part of the job, but at least, he could be a little more casual.

He spotted Rae pulling a weed from one of the many flowerbeds.

"You know we have a fairly skilled staff of gardeners to take care of that kind of thing," he said, heading toward his wife.

Rae laughed. "I know, I know. I just can't help myself. I've been puttering around out here for half an hour. It's beautiful."

"As are you," said James, stealing a kiss. "Now that it's warming up, I try to take a walk out here at least once a day."

"Do you ever run into Dolley Madison?" asked Rae.

James thought for a moment. "As in James Madison's wife?"

Rae nodded.

"She was the one who originally planted this garden, right?"

Rae nodded again.

"You're about to tell me another ghost story, right?"

"Yes, I am," Rae laughed. "I've been researching White House hauntings. Apparently first lady, Ellen Wilson, ordered that the garden be dug up in the early 1900s, but the ghost of Dolley Madison spooked her, and the garden stayed. Rumor has it she can still be seen out here among the roses."

James grinned. "I would love to putter around out here with you, and say hello to Dolley, but duty calls."

"What's up today?"

159

"I'm meeting with Dr. Lakey about the Japanese plan to offer the Hecatians alternative sites for their habitation."

"Has everyone agreed on the sites?" asked Rae.

"For the most part, we settled on two, Ayers Rock and the Canada/Montana combination. The Australians and the Canadians were very willing to help. I had more trouble with the Montana folks. Their Lieutenant Governor was insistent that the Federal Government was constitutionally prohibited from annexing their land."

"How did you convince them?"

"I reminded him that I was annexing about 500 square miles, while the alien's original plan would annex his entire state."

"How many people live in that area?"

"A couple thousand," said James. "We committed to relocating them. Same with those that would be impacted in Canada and Australia."

"Have you figured out how to communicate this plan to the aliens?"

"That's part of this discussion, which I'm late for. See you later."

As Rae set her sights on another flowerbed, the President entered the West Wing and headed straight for the Roosevelt Room.

Kyle Lakey stood as the President entered the room. He was dressed in a suit and tie.

"Thanks for coming in," said Martin. "Feel free to lose that jacket and tie. It is Saturday."

Lakey seemed conflicted for a moment, then slipped off his suit coat and loosened his tie.

Martin smiled and sat down across the table from the doctor. "Have you figured out how to speak Hecatian?"

"Yes, Mr. President, in a way we have." Lakey tapped a couple of buttons on the conference table and two images were projected on a screen. "The graphic on the left is a two-dimensional rendering of the global view from the Hecatian grey screen which showed the alien's proposed respirator locations. We've matched the grey background, purple symbols, and markings as close as possible to the screens. We assume the Hecatians will recognize this."

Lakey tapped a button and a large red X appeared over the first image.

The President nodded. "Ah, the universal symbol for 'not gonna happen.'"

"That's right. At least we hope it's universal," said Lakey, pointing to the other side of the screen. "The image on the right is a map of the northwest United States and southwest Canada. We used the same color scheme. You can see that we have highlighted the proposed alien habitation site and placed the respirator symbol on the highest elevated structures. We believe the Hecatians will interpret this as an alternative proposal because the respirator sites are different from their original plans."

Lakey clicked again, and a third image appeared with the Australian site depicted in a similar manner. "As you know, Ayers Rock was one of the alien's original respirator sites. We still think they will understand that we are offering a reduced section of central Australia as an alternative site."

"How do we deliver the message?"

"That's much more complicated, but we have some good ideas. Are you familiar with the messages that NASA sent into space as part of the Pioneer and Voyager projects in the 1970s?"

"Sure. They had metal space maps showing how to find Earth. Later missions carried a greeting in several different languages."

"That's right. The last couple of Pioneer probes had metal plaques attached to them with pictures etched on them. The Voyager probes carried gold-plated copper discs with images and sounds from Earth. The discs included recordings in 55 languages."

"I remember now," said Martin. "They all said 'Hello from the children of planet Earth.' "

"Actually, that was just the English message. Each country submitted a different message. Most were simple greetings, or messages of peace. Oddly, the Chinese message was 'Have you eaten yet?'"

Martin laughed. "You can't be serious."

"I'm totally serious. I've always wondered what they were thinking."

"And sixty years later, we're still wondering what they are thinking."

"There was also music and other nature sounds like rain, thunder and crickets," Lakey continued. "They even included a diagram of human DNA as they understood it back then."

"But there's no solid evidence that those messages ever reached anything out there," said the President.

"That's true, but they were just randomly rocketing these messages into space. We've got something to aim at."

The President put both hands behind his head and stretched back in his chair. "So we are going to strap all of this stuff to a spacedrone and fire it at the asteroid?"

Lakey shook his head. "That's the best part. We've got better ways of delivering the message then they had 60 years ago. We've given this the codename Dove."

"As in the bird?"

"Yes. In the biblical story of the flood, a dove delivered an olive branch to Noah, signifying that the water was receding. Shortly thereafter, the ark came to rest on dry land."

"I like the symbolism," said the President. "But I assume you're not planning to wrap our proposal around an olive branch."

Lakey laughed. "No, sir. We've got something more technical in mind."

"Go on."

"You get e-mail messages all day long, with text, and sound, and images. How do those messages come to you?"

"Most of them come through this thing," said Martin, pointing to his PIB.

"Exactly. Wireless files sent through cyberspace."

"You mean we can send the Hecatians a text message?" asked Martin.

"Sort of. The files will be bigger, but basically it's the same technology."

"What kind of files?"

"All of them. Just like the Voyager probes that carried messages in multiple languages. We will send our message in every computerized file type that we have."

"And they will be able to read them?"

Lakey nodded. "With their advanced technology, definitely. They have most likely been monitoring us for a long time. At first it would have been radio and television broadcasts. So we will definitely send our messages in those formats. In the last several decades, they would be picking up our Internet traffic. We will send files in Virtual Reality Modeling Language which is most common for Internet communication. But we will also send file types that were more prevalent during the early part of this century, like bitmap and vector."

"How long will it take these messages to reach the asteroid?" asked Martin.

"Not as fast as they travel on Earth, but still pretty quick. We will be tapping into some of the laser-guided satellite technology that we use to track and monitor the asteroid."

"I'm not going to pretend that I understand all of this Dr. Lakey. But you obviously have a good grasp of things. You also seem pretty confident that this will work."

"I'm 100 percent confident that we can get the message to them. And, I believe they will be able to read it. I'm just not sure how they will respond."

163

"That is the big unknown," said the President as he rose and left the room. A second later, he stuck his head back through the door. "Let's just hope they've already eaten."

CHAPTER 45

Tuesday, May 5, 2037
The White House

Three minutes into his meeting with the White House Budget Coordinator, President Martin started rapidly tapping his knee with a pen. Ten seconds later, Gwen Hardin knocked lightly on the Oval Office door.

"I'm sorry to interrupt, Mr. President. General Bolser and Secretary Turner need a moment with you."

"Thank you, Gwen" Martin rose from the sofa and shook his visitor's hand. "And thank you for your time. I will review these numbers and get back to you."

Martin eyed Craig Bolser and Jordyn Turner as they entered the room. "You two are a dangerous combination. I am going to guess that China has complicated matters further."

Turner nodded. "Good guess."

"About a half-hour ago, Premier Feng publically announced that they will be launching a nuclear-armed spacedrone early next month," said Bolser. "He also said this action was the only viable alternative to ensure the protection of the Chinese Republic, and the planet."

Secretary Turner added, "Within minutes of the announcement, North Korea, Iraq and Syria released statements in support of the Chinese plan."

The President ran his fingers through his hair and released a long sigh. "What's the likelihood they can pull this off?"

"There is no doubt that their drones have the capability of reaching the asteroid," said Bolser. "And their nuclear armaments are as advanced as our own. The question is if they can combine the two. Chinese spacedrones have traditionally carried a very limited payload. A warhead and the associated detonation mechanism will be a challenge for them."

"They may have been working on that capability without our knowledge," said Martin.

"That is a possibility, Mr. President," said Bolser.

Martin thought for a moment. "Maybe we should let them try this. If it works, our problems are solved. If it fails, there's really no harm done."

"That's one way of looking at it," said Bolser. "But there are some other things that need to be considered."

"What's that?" asked Martin.

The General activated his PIB and pulled-up a three-dimensional model of the solar system. "Shortly after we learned of China's armed spacedrone plan, we began to track the path of 29075 DA, relative to Earth's orbit around the sun. The asteroid's path merges with our planet's orbital path for roughly five days in late June. We have never been concerned with this because it would be a few months before the Earth would reach that point in orbit. The asteroid would have moved well-inside our orbital path at that point."

Bolser paused as the President reviewed the model.

"I follow you," said Martin. "So what's the concern?"

"If China follows through with their plan to launch in early June, it is very likely they would reach the asteroid during that five-day window. If they are successful in destroying the asteroid with a nuclear device, it would create a massive amount of dangerous debris. Earth would pass right through that debris field months later."

"And that debris would pose a danger to the planet?" asked Martin.

Bolser nodded. "Yes it would. But even more concerning is the radiation field that would be created. Even if they miss the asteroid completely, a detonation would pose a big danger."

"Wouldn't the radiation dissipate by the time the Earth moved into the area?" asked Turner.

"Possibly," said Bolser. "We know that material dissipates slower in space than it does in Earth's atmosphere. We assume there would still be some level of radiation present, but we aren't certain how much, or how damaging it would be."

"So we either face exposure to deadly radiation, or exposure to deadly radiation with asteroid debris," said Turner.

"That's right," said the President. "And, there's a third scenario we haven't mentioned. If they hit the asteroid, but don't destroy the Hecatians, we will have radiation, debris, and a swarm of angry aliens waiting for us."

Turner's eyes widened. "Surely the Chinese have considered all of this."

"Maybe they have, maybe they haven't," said Bolser. "Either way, it's clear they see no other alternative."

The trio stared quietly at the holographic model.

"Let's give them an alternative," said Martin.

"What do you have in mind?" asked Bolser.

"We've kept Project Dove under wraps. If we go public with this strategy, along with the flaws in the Chinese plan, we might generate enough support to pressure China into reconsidering the launch."

"I like it," said Turner.

"So do I," said Bolser. "I'll get with Kyle Lakey and start working on a press conference."

The President raised his hand, interrupting Bolser. "I definitely want you and Dr. Lakey involved. But this announcement should come from Japan. This was their idea. We have partnered with them, along with Australia and Canada."

"A global solution," said the General.

"Exactly, General, a global solution," said Martin as he turned his attention to Jordyn Turner. "Madame Secretary, we need to ensure that some of our allies are willing to jump on our bandwagon right after this announcement is made."

"That won't be a problem," said Turner. "The European Union has been very vocal in their opposition to a nuclear option."

"Good," said Martin. "Let's make this happen."

CHAPTER 46

The town car pulled alongside the curb just long enough for Rudolph Overton to step out onto the sidewalk. He took a seat on a nearby park bench. From here he had a perfect view of the White House.

Years ago, when he was younger, Overton would begin almost every work day by sitting on this bench, looking at the White House. After a few minutes, he would walk the 10 blocks to the Federal Trade Commission.

As time passed, and the walk grew longer, his visits to the bench became fewer and fewer. Still, he managed the routine at least twice a month now.

Decades ago, he could have walked right up to the White House door. Pennsylvania Avenue was now much wider. And there were fences and barricades, and guards, both seen and unseen, between him and the mansion.

The view, however, was still the same. As was the fire in Overton's belly; the burning hatred that rekindled every time he sat on this bench. Every visit, which now numbered in the thousands, reminded him of his purpose and reinforced his resolve.

His inner inferno was intensified this morning. Yesterday's news that China would strike the asteroid in June was an unexpected, yet welcome, surprise. Overton did not think for a moment that they would be able to reach the asteroid, let alone destroy it. But that did not matter. The spacedrone had already accomplished its mission by creating chaos for the United States.

Overton grinned as he imagined the conversations that had to have taken place in the White House yesterday. What would the President do now? Will he flex his military might? Will he back down? Or will he create yet another story, rooted in lies and deceit? Regardless, the President will have to do something. He can longer ignore the issue and sit idly by in a self-created, ignorant bliss.

"Your move, Mr. President," whispered Overton. "Your move."

CHAPTER 47

Wednesday, May 6, 2037
The White House

Just past 10 p.m., President Martin was alone in his study in the White House residence. He was trying to catch-up on reading the virtual mountain of briefs that had stacked up on his PIB.

Rae would be in New York overnight, meeting with the Red Cross on the gas mask project. The White House always felt like a big empty museum at night. That feeling was magnified when Rae was away.

Martin thought he might be able to focus better in the Oval Office, and he was certain the walk would do him good. As he headed down the residence hallway, he ran into Chris Boone.

"Good evening, Mr. President."

"Hello, Agent Boone. Why the late night?"

"I like to take a night-shift every now and then. It gives me a chance to catch-up with the rest of the team," said Boone. "Is there anything I can help you with?"

"No, just thought I'd go for a run," said Martin, increasing his walking pace.

"A run, sir?" asked Boone, with an obvious strain in his voice.

Martin laughed. "Just as far as the West Wing. Have a good night, Agent Boone."

Boone shook his head and mumbled something under his breath.

Pleased with himself for agitating the man that was responsible for keeping him alive, Martin tapped his PIB and placed a phone call.

Deanna Faye answered on the second ring. "Hi, Jimmy."

"Hello, Sis. Am I interrupting?"

"Goodness, no. Paul's watching TV. I'm reading."

"How was dad today?"

"Pretty much the same," said Deanna. "He's asking about mom less now, just a couple times today."

In the days after their mother's death, James and his sister had agreed to do everything possible to allow their father to stay in his home. This included hiring homecare staff to be with him around-the-clock. Joe Martin was still capable of taking care of himself, but he reluctantly agreed to the extra help.

"How is he getting along with the nursing staff?" asked James.

"He's friendly with them most of the time. But he always makes a point of telling me that he doesn't need them."

"Did you get the information I sent?"

"Yes, but Jimmy, he's never going to agree to move to a nursing home, let alone one in D.C."

James sighed. "I know he won't like it. But we're getting close to the point that we need to do what's best for him, regardless of his wishes."

"I agree," said Deanna. "But, I don't think moving halfway across the country is what's best for him."

James reached the Oval Office and sat down behind his desk. "But Joplin doesn't have a true Alzheimer's care center. The facilities here are..."

Deanna interrupted. "He's doesn't need a facility of any kind. When he is no longer safe in his home, he will move in here."

"You shouldn't have to take that on Deanna."

"He's my dad," said Deanna. "I think it is my responsibility to take care of him."

"But he's my dad, too. It's as much my responsibility as it is yours."

"You're a little busy, James. You do have a fairly important job."

"So do you, Sis. Running that library is a fulltime commitment."

"You're right. It's a lot of hours, but much of what I do can be done from home. And don't forget that Paul is retired. He's here all the time."

James didn't respond. He knew she was right.

"I know this is hard for you, Jimmy. I know you want to fix this. You've spent your whole life fixing things. But you can't fix dad."

James wiped a tear from his cheek. "I feel like I've abandoned him."

"OK. But you know deep down that you haven't abandoned him. I know that. He knows that too."

James fell silent again.

"Do you remember those long talks you had with mom, getting her to accept dad's situation? Everything you told her applies to you now. You just have to accept the situation we're in."

James let out a breath. "You're right, as usual."

Deanna laughed. "It's like I tell Paul, if you would just listen to me the first time, we would save a lot of effort."

"I should find you a position on my staff."

"Oh, no you shouldn't," said Deanna. "I'll leave running the country to you, little brother."

"I love you, Sis. I'll talk to you soon."

"Love you too."

James reached for a family picture that was sitting on the credenza behind his desk. Mom and dad, Deanna and Paul, Rae and him, were all smiles on his parent's front porch. It had been taken just after the election, and was the last picture of the family together.

That was just six months ago, he thought. *So much had happened since then, mom's death, the aliens...*

He looked at the closet door. He had been avoiding it for weeks. Somewhere deep in his gut, between the sorrow and the guilt, he felt something pulling. Giving into the temptation, he made his way to the closet, through the door, and past the flags.

The room was much like before, chairs, tables, warm fire, knickknacks on the mantle. He took a step toward the center of the room and spotted the bottom step of the stairway at the end of the wall. Moving closer to the fire, he noticed a framed picture above the mantle. It was a painting of Mortimer, similar in style to the presidential portraits that adorned the wall of the White House. Mortimer was wearing his familiar brown suit. His deep blue eyes bulged from the canvas, as if they were about to blink.

"Ah, Mr. President, I thought I might see you tonight." Mortimer was sitting behind Martin, motioning to an empty chair. "Please do sit down."

Martin sat down, facing Mortimer, as the fireplace crackled. The look on Mortimer's face was an exact match to the portrait. The only difference was his host's steady blinking.

"What can I do for you?" asked Mortimer.

"I'm not sure," said Martin. "I was just feeling a bit lost tonight, I guess."

Mortimer smiled knowingly. "It is funny that one can be heading in the right direction and still feel as if they are lost."

Martin slowly shook his head. "I don't follow you."

"Just because you *feel* lost, does not necessarily mean that you *are* lost," said Mortimer.

"Or you could just be missin' your sweetheart," said Emma. She was sitting in a chair, next to Mortimer, knitting a sweater which was almost complete. The puppercat was dozing in Emma's lap, wearing the unfinished sweater.

Mortimer closed his eyes. "Emma."

"Yes, Morty," said Emma.

"I thought you had retired for the evening."

"And miss this? No way. Besides, I needed some coffee." Emma reached for one of three cups that had appeared on a table. Each was already filled with steaming liquid and swirling with cream. "Have some coffee dear."

Martin reached for a cup. "Is it decaf?"

"De-what?" said Emma, with a curious blink.

"Decaffeinated," said Martin. "It's pretty late."

Emma looked completely stumped. "Why would anyone drink decaffeinated coffee?"

Martin looked toward Mortimer for help, but he was already lost in his swirls. "You're right. This is fine."

The three sat in silence for a moment, sipping and swirling. Martin noticed that the picture above the fireplace was now a portrait of Emma, holding a single rose.

"Emma, how often do you get out to the Rose Garden?" asked Martin.

Emma froze, mid-sip. She peered over her cup, first at Martin, then at Mortimer, and then back at Martin.

Mortimer slowly sipped his coffee, waiting patiently for Emma's answer.

"Not very often, since the incident," said Emma.

"The incident?" asked Martin.

Emma looked toward Mortimer for help.

"There was some…excitement…in the Rose Garden some years ago, when Emma stuck her nose where it didn't belong," explained Mortimer.

"What better place to stick your nose than in a rose garden," said Emma. "Besides, that woman was absolutely batty thinking she was going to dig up my roses. I mean *those* roses."

Martin nodded. He was starting to understand things better now.

"You were talking about people feeling lost," said Martin, coaxing Mortimer out of his trance.

"Indeed," said Mortimer. "The challenge is to resist the urge to change direction, merely as a reaction to feeling lost."

"What if you're not going anywhere? Wouldn't you need to change direction then?"

"Possibly," said Mortimer. "But, first, consider that you may not be going anywhere because you are already exactly where you need to be."

The President nodded.

Emma snorted. "Do you think if I start drinking decaf, I'll understand this guy any better? 'Cuz sometimes he's like talking to a fortune cookie."

Martin stood, in an effort to hide the smile on his face. He did not want to offend Mortimer, but he had to admit, Emma's comment was funny.

"I think I will leave you two to the rest of your evening," said Martin. "I enjoyed our talk, thank you."

"Anytime, Mr. President," said Mortimer and Emma together.

CHAPTER 48

James Martin slipped into bed after a very long day. If he was lucky, he might get six hours of sleep tonight. Before turning off the bedside light, he leaned over to kiss his wife. He bolted upright, throwing off the covers.

Rae was lying on her back, perfectly still, wearing a gas mask. The muffled giggles started almost immediately.

"What in the world are you doing?" asked James, as his heart rate returned to normal.

Still laughing, Rae removed the mask. "Dennis Gordon sent over a few of these today. What do you think?"

James examined the mask. "I've always said you look great in anything. This might be the exception."

"I think it's kind of stylish."

James pulled the mask over his face and looked at his wife.

"Ok, maybe not."

"It sure didn't take them long to produce this," said James.

"This is just a prototype. Dr. Gordon's team is going to do one more round of testing before they green-light the mass production."

"That's great. We're making real progress. We just need to figure out how to distribute them."

Rae grinned. "We're making progress in that area, too. Gwen Hardin said you were hoping Santa could help us."

"Just trying to think outside the box a little," said James.

"Well, Santa's not available. But, according to Gwen, one of his elves works for us."

"Who's that?"

"Aaron Ash," said Rae. "He has worked with almost every country in existence, organizing state dinners and other White House activities. He says the best contact for this type of shipping and logistics project is our own embassy in each country. He gave me a long list of contacts that I passed on to the Red Cross."

"But we don't have embassies in every country."

"Mr. Ash has that covered too. He's well-connected with all the global shipping companies and has been for decades. If he doesn't have a direct contact in a country, he knows someone who does."

James nodded enthusiastically. "This is great news."

The first lady rolled her eyes.

"What?" he asked.

"Take the stupid mask off, James. It's very hard to take you seriously with that thing flopping around."

James pulled the mask over his face, but left it sitting on top of his head. "Hey, you started this."

Rae sighed. *"J'aurais dû savoir mieux que vous donner un nouveau jouet si près de votre heure du coucher."*

James thought for a moment. "You said something about me being the sexiest man alive."

"Not quite," said Rae. "I said, I should have known better than to give you a new toy so close to your bedtime."

CHAPTER 49

Friday, May 15, 2037
The White House

The Briefing Room was filled beyond capacity. Cameras hummed and clicked. Reporters jostled for position.

President Martin stood behind the podium, flanked by Kyle Lakey. The President had spent the last 15 minutes responding to questions related to Project Dove.

Earlier in the day, representatives from the Japanese government and Japan's Aerospace Exploration Program had held a press conference detailing the plan. The announcement included extensive information about the Ayers Rock site in Australia as well as the combined US-Canadian site. The communication plan was outlined, including examples of the maps and virtual models that would be sent to the Hecatians. June 8 was announced as the day the communication transmissions would begin.

In his opening remarks, President Martin had praised the Japanese space program for coming up with the alternative site idea. He also acknowledged Dr. Lakey, and the Majestic team, for partnering with Japan to bring the plan to fruition. He closed by thanking Australia, Canada and the State of Montana for their cooperation.

Martin had opened the question-and-answer portion of the press conference by calling on reporters who had agreed to ask specifically-scripted questions in exchange for their moment in the spotlight. This allowed the President to emphasize additional key points about the plan.

The President's communication staff had decided not to plant every key question with reporters in advance, assuming that certain topics would be raised without prompting. So far, the random questions from journalists had given the President the opportunity to cover all of his important talking-points, except for the most important one.

Martin pointed to an energetic reporter in the back of the room who had been standing on her tip-toes and waving frantically throughout the meeting.

"How does this plan impact China's intention to launch an armed spacedrone, targeting the asteroid, later this month?"

Bingo, Martin thought to himself.

He let the question hang in the air for a few seconds. "We don't know for certain, but our hope is that China will consider this plan to be a viable alternative to their military option."

Martin then turned the room over to Kyle Lakey to answer some of the more technical questions that the President had deferred earlier.

Alan Kingman was waiting in the hallway as the President exited the room.

"How did that sound?" asked Martin.

"Right on target," said Kingman. "Canada and Australia are starting their press conferences now. Other countries will be releasing statements of support throughout the rest of the day."

"How about England?" asked the President.

"I talked with Secretary Turner an hour ago. She said the Prime Minister has agreed to address the flaws in the Chinese spacedrone plan in a press conference first thing in the morning. He has the orbital path model and will emphasize the radiation and debris danger."

"Excellent," said Martin. "Let's see how Premier Feng responds to a little outside pressure."

CHAPTER 50

Thursday, May 28, 2037
The White House

President Martin leaned forward and rubbed his temples. He was just five minutes into a telephone conversation with the Chinese Premier, Feng Li Bo. His head was pounding, and his patience was growing thin.

It was 8:35 p.m. in Washington and 8:35 a.m. in Beijing. Despite President Martin's willingness to accommodate the Chinese leader's schedule, Premier Feng had, thus far, been rather unaccommodating on the call.

Officially, this was a *private* phone call between two of the most powerful people on the planet. But Martin suspected that members of Premier Feng's staff were listening in on the call, which was exactly why General Bolser, Secretary Turner and Chief of Staff Kingman were seated with the President in the Oval Office.

The four were all fixated on the glasstop screen which sat atop the coffee table in the middle of the room. Premier Feng could be heard faintly in the background speaking Mandarin. A computer translated the conversation into English. Feng was working with a similar system which translated President's Martin's comments into Mandarin.

Martin's tone, while cordial at the beginning of the call, was growing noticeably tighter.

"Premier Feng, you said a few weeks ago that you felt your armed spacedrone was the only viable option available to protect your people. We believe the alternative site plan provides you with a viable option. Most of the countries in the United Nations agree."

"Puppets!" said Feng. "Those other countries are merely puppets, and the United States is the puppeteer. They agree with you because you tell them to agree with you. It has been this way for decades."

"Are you saying the alternative site plan is not a viable option?" asked Martin.

"I am saying that our plan ensures the security of the planet. Your Project Dove is nothing more than a prayer."

"What about the British Prime Minister's concerns about the potential debris and radiation fallout?"

"It may have been the Prime Minister's mouth that was moving, but it was clearly your words, President Martin. And do you arrogant Americans truly believe that you are the only nation capable of making these assessments?"

"So you believe your plan is safe?" asked Martin.

"There will be no debris because we will turn that rock into gravel. The radiation will go away before the Earth reaches that part of its orbit."

"And your drone is capable of reaching the asteroid in time?"

"Most definitely," said Feng. "We have more than enough time."

"Then what is the harm in pushing your launch date back a few weeks? Let us send the message to the Hecatians. Give them some time to respond. If they do not, then launch your missile."

Feng was silent for a moment. "Do you have any other requests, Mr. President?"

"Not at this time," said Martin.

Feng ended the call.

Alan Kingman stood and started pacing. "Pardon my English, but that guy was talking out of his ass. There's no way they considered the radiation fallout."

"I agree," said General Bolser. "If they really have that wide of a launch window, they would avoid the orbital path."

"He did not sound too enthusiastic about your proposal, Mr. President," said Turner. "What do you think he will do?"

Martin thought for a moment. "I think his scientists will eventually find the courage to tell him they agree with the radiation risk, and I think he will then move back his launch date."

"I agree," said Kingman, starting a second lap around the room. "But he won't tell us that."

"No, he won't, but that's OK," said Martin, glancing at the closet door. "We are not going to alter our plans regardless of what he does, because we are moving in the right direction."

CHAPTER 51

Monday, June 8, 2037
The White House

The military helicopter touched down perfectly on the landing pads as the President watched from the door to the South Lawn. As the rotors slowed, Martin stepped onto the patio and waited for Alan Kingman to emerge from the chopper.

A minute later, the Chief of Staff joined Martin on the patio. Kingman looked around. Aside from the flight crew, there was no one else in sight.

"Why is it that when you land here there's a throng of reporters and half of the White House staff standing around? I get nothing."

Martin raised an eyebrow. "The President of the United States is holding the door open for you. What more could you ask for?"

Kingman thought for a moment. "How about fire trucks and a marching band?"

"How about you fill me in on your trip to the Pentagon?" said Martin, stepping inside.

The President had sent Kingman to observe the commencement of Project Dove. A team from NASA, and a large contingent from Japan, had joined the Majestic team. Martin felt a member of the executive branch should be present to show support.

"To be honest, it was kind of anti-climactic," said Kingman. "They spent half-an-hour confirming that the various file formats were in place. It was a lot like the go-no-go they do before a space launch. Then they waited for the appointed time and pressed the enter button on a virtual keyboard."

"Seriously," said Martin, "one button?"

Kingman nodded. "One button. Everyone clapped and cheered, and then they wheeled in a giant cake."

"I don't suppose the Hecatians responded immediately," said Martin.

"No, nothing yet," said Kingman. "The joke was that the aliens would probably just phone you directly."

"As crazy as the last few months have been, that would not surprise me a bit," said Martin.

"General Bolser asked me to pass along an update on the Chinese spacedrone."

"Good news, I hope."

"Yes," said Kingman. "Bolser said our satellite video shows a high level of activity around the launch site, but they have yet to move the spacedrone into position. He says this mean they are at least a week away from being ready to launch."

"Does that mean the asteroid would be out of Earth's orbital path before they could reach it?"

Kingman nodded. "Yes. The General confirmed that."

"Excellent, that's one less thing to worry about."

Gwen Hardin intercepted the President as they reached the Oval Office.

"I have General Bolser holding for you."

"Thank you Gwen." Martin motioned Kingman into the room. He tapped the phone icon on the desk glasstop.

"Hello, General. Alan was just giving me the good news about China."

"Yes, Mr. President" said Bolser. "And I'm calling with more good news. Kyle Lakey just informed me that we have received confirmation that the Project Dove files have reached the asteroid and have been opened by the Hecatians."

"How can we tell they have opened them?" asked Martin.

"According to Dr. Lakey, each file was embedded with code that would transmit a signal back to us whenever the file was opened. It's similar to a read receipt on an e-mail."

"Which format were they able to open?" asked Martin.

"All of them," said Bolser. "Apparently we underestimated their capabilities."

Martin looked at Kingman who was shaking his head in amazement. "Apparently so…do you see any harm in releasing this information to the media?"

"As long as we are careful not to represent this as a response from the Hecatians, I see no harm in it," said Bolser.

"I agree," said Kingman. "This news should give everyone a lift."

"General, is Dr. Lakey still there?" asked Martin.

"I believe he is," said Bolser.

"Good," said Martin. "Tell him I said congratulations. Then stick him in front of a television camera."

CHAPTER 52

Wednesday, June 24, 2037
The White House

Premier Feng stood rigid in front of several television cameras. Behind him was a launch pad with a swarm of military vehicles moving in and out of frame. A spacedrone, emblazoned with a large Chinese flag, was attached to the launch tower. Workers were detaching a cable that was connected to a massive crane.

An unseen reporter translated Feng's comments into English. "The American plan has failed. It has been more than two weeks. The aliens have not responded. The Republic of China will strike to protect our people and our planet."

President Martin tapped the glasstop on his desk to turn off the television. He turned to Craig Bolser who was standing next to the desk, almost as rigid as Feng.

"They moved the drone to the launch pad overnight," said the General. "We are reviewing the satellite footage to determine if the armaments have already been loaded. We assume they have not, as it is safer to do so after the drone is attached to the tower."

"Assuming they have not armed the drone, how soon could they launch?" asked Martin.

"About five days," said Bolser.

"And if it is already armed?"

"Three," said Bolser.

The President leaned back in his chair and ran his fingers through his hair. "Any chance we have just failed to pick up the Hecatians response?"

Bolser shook his head. "Not with the equipment we have aimed at that asteroid. If they had sent any kind of transmission, we would have picked it up."

"Feng has delayed three weeks from his original launch date," said Martin. "I don't know how we could stop him now."

Bolser started to speak, but hesitated.

"What is it, General?"

"Mr. President, we can take out that launch site in less than an hour."

"I know we can. But Feng would consider that an act of war. We have enough to deal with already."

"I agree, sir," said Bolser. "I just wanted to go on record with the option."

"The way I see it, we have no choice but to sit back and watch this," said Martin. "Feng just might pull it off."

CHAPTER 53

Saturday, June 27, 2037
Hanover County, VA

Skip McGee strained to hear the music from the band shell across the park. He did not want to miss his cue.

He had been prepping for several days–packing charges, loading fuses, mapping alignments. This was his first solo operations assignment. His boss was working a different job at the other end of the state. Skip would be working the big displays with his boss every night for the next week. That was assuming he didn't screw up this show.

This was a small gig by comparison, about 100 units, or 15 minutes worth of pyro. Hanover County always held its Independence Day celebration on the Saturday before July 4th, because everyone in town went to Richmond for the big show on the fourth.

Skip had spent the afternoon unpacking the cylinders and loading them into the launch racks. He was careful to confirm the color loads and altitude settings. He had been a little confused by the extra cylinder in the finale crate, but he knew the boss often threw in an extra bang or two, especially for the smaller shows and the repeat customers. He wired the extra tube into the middle of the finale package. No problem, the last package launched from a singled fuse. Everything was preset with lots and lots of bang.

The crowd was singing the Star Spangled Banner. Skip wiped his hands on his jeans and checked the connection on the firing box one last time. Everything looked perfect.

...and the rockets' red glare... Skip flipped the first fuse. Streams of bright red fire shot high into the air.

...the bombs bursting in air... loud reports sounded as the red streams reached there apex.

Skip grinned as he waited for his next cue. This may have been the ultimate firework cliché, but it was still seriously cool.

A few seconds later, the crowd grew louder as the anthem ended with *...the home of the brave!...* Skip threw the next fuse as the band started playing *Yankee Doodle-Dandy*. A series of rockets shot up from the launch rack, followed by dazzling bursts of fire and light.

Skip could no longer hear the music over the hissing rockets and loud explosions, but it didn't matter. The rest of the show was all based on timing. Directly under each fuse on his firing box was a piece of masking tape with a number written on it. Skip would hit the fuse, silently count to the number on the tape, and then hit the next fuse.

One, two, three, four...GO!...One, two, three, four, five...GO!...

He was always amazed at how fast this part of the show went. Ten minutes later, he was nearing his final fuse.

He could hear the crowd roaring and cheering as the intensity of the display increased. They were anticipating the finale.

Skip fired the last fuse and looked up to savor the pinnacle of his masterpiece. His eyes widened as an ocean of light filled the sky. A barrage of explosions echoed with such force that he could feel it in his chest.

He barely had time to realize that something was abnormal before a searing white light scorched his eyes and set his face on fire.

CHAPTER 54

James and Rae Martin snuggled together on a comfy sofa in the White House residence, watching a movie and sharing a bowl of popcorn.

One of the perks of the office was being able to get a private screening of just about any film. This used to be the Martin's favorite downtime activity, but in the last few months they rarely made it to the end of the movie. Either they were interrupted, or they both fell asleep.

Tonight, they were thirty minutes into a romantic comedy that Rae had selected. So far, both the President and the first lady were still awake.

The President's PIB buzzed. Rae hit the pause button on the remote. The President sat the popcorn bowl on the table and fingered the glowing YAK icon.

"This better be good," said the President.

"Is it ever good when I call you on the weekend?" said Kingman.

"No. What's up?"

"There's been an accident at a public fireworks display in Hanover County, Virginia. We don't have specifics yet, but it sounds like some rockets went into the crowd. There are some fatalities and a lot of injuries."

"Did you say it was a public event?" asked Martin. "Isn't it a little early for that?"

"No. Lots of smaller towns have early celebrations because they lose their citizens to bigger cities on the fourth," said Kingman.

191

"Let me know when you have more details, or if you need me to make some calls to route more help down there."

"We are trying to get ahold of Virginia's Governor right now," said Kingman. "I'll call you if we hit any roadblocks."

Martin disconnected the call.

"I always worry about that happening at those kinds of displays," said Rae. "Large crowds and fireworks seem like a dangerous combination."

James reached for the popcorn. "You're right, but there are few things more American than a big fireworks display. Fortunately, these kinds of accidents are pretty rare."

Rae restarted the movie and couple settled back into the sofa.

A half-hour later, the President's PIB buzzed again.

It was Kingman again. This time his voice was firmer. "We have reports of two more incidents at public fireworks displays in Maine and New Hampshire."

"That can't be a coincidence," said the President.

"Not a chance," said Kingman. "Bolser is on his way. We are gathering in the Situation Room."

"I'll be right there," said Martin.

Moments later General Bolser and the President arrived at the Situation Room. A trio of military communication specialists was seated along one wall, typing furiously and talking into headsets. Alan Kingman was standing in front of a bank of television screens. Feeds from three different news sources were displayed.

"What do we have?" asked the President.

Kingman kept his eyes locked on the screens. "In addition to the Virginia site, there have been similar occurrences in Meredith, New Hampshire and Rockland, Maine."

Each news channel was broadcasting a montage of video clips showing emergency vehicles, rescue personnel, and civilians tending to the injured. Most of the victims being shown had burns to the eyes or face.

"It's hard to describe," said a witness on one of the channels. "It was a very white, very hot light. It lasted a few seconds, and then was gone."

The President turned to General Bolser. "Any ideas?"

Bolser shook his head. "Not really, some of the injuries look like chemical burns, but that doesn't explain the white light."

"Alan, any word yet on the number of casualties?" asked Martin.

"We can tell from monitoring the emergency frequencies that there have been fatalities at each location," said Kingman, pointing to the screens. "Obviously there are a lot of injuries as well."

"And we are certain this isn't a coincidence?" asked Martin.

"Absolutely not, Mr. President," said Bolser. "There are accidents at fireworks displays every year, but not to this extent. Plus, the eye-witness accounts at each location are very similar. This is definitely a coordinated attack."

Martin continued to watch the video screens. One of the networks had added a graphic above the video that read, "Deadly Display."

"Do we have any idea how many other communities have firework displays scheduled for tonight?" asked Martin.

One of the communication specialists removed her headset and swiveled her chair. "We've been running Internet searches and have turned up six other events so far."

"There has to be more than that," said Kingman.

General Bolser checked the long line of digital clocks on the far wall, each displayed the current time for a specific time zone. "It is 10:40 p.m. here and 9:40 p.m. in the Central time zone. The optimal start time for a fireworks display is between 9:45 and 10:15 p.m."

"So there will be another round of displays starting any time," said Kingman.

"Bring up a current national weather map," said Bolser.

"Screen 6, sir," said one of the specialists.

Bolser stepped to the screen. The center section of the country was covered with green and yellow blobs. "Most of the central time zone is getting rain right now. That helps. Unfortunately, the mountain region and west coast are clear."

"Alan, I am issuing an executive order prohibiting all public and private firework displays, effective immediately. How soon can we get the word out?"

Kingman looked at a specialist who was already typing.

"Very quickly," said Kingman.

Martin and Kingman continued to monitor the news channels while General Bolser made phone calls to coordinate an initial investigation.

After a few minutes, one of the news feeds cut to a studio anchor. "The White House has just released a statement indicating that President Martin has issued an executive order prohibiting all firework displays, both public and private, effective immediately."

Kingman fingered through several websites on his PIB.

"It's all over the Internet," said Kingman. "That should shut everything down."

CHAPTER 55

Sunday, June 28, 2037
The White House

President Martin returned to the Situation Room shortly after 7:30 a.m. General Bolser and Alan Kingman had arrived an hour before. All three had called it a night just after 1 a.m., when they had confirmed that all of the west coast firework displays had been cancelled.

Three video screens displayed coverage of the previous night's incidents from different news sources. A fourth screen was a feed from a Chinese broadcast showing the spacedrone on the launch pad.

"What's happening in China?" asked Martin.

"There has been a flurry of activity in the last several hours," said Bolser. "We think they are arming the drone and making final launch preparations."

Kingman pointed to a different screen. "This could have something to do with the spacedrone activity."

General Wilbert Knudsen was being interviewed on one of the morning talk shows. "Obviously these attacks were coordinated. Based on the unusual type of weapon that was deployed, we have to at least consider that this could have originated with the Hecatians, perhaps in response to Project Dove."

Kingman hit the mute button and turned to the President. "Since when did that crap weasel become our spokesman? That's the third interview he's given this morning, and it's not even eight yet."

"Any guess where Knudsen is getting his info, General Bolser?" asked Martin.

"I have no idea," said Bolser. "FBI and ATF personnel worked through the night at each location. At this point, they have very little to go on. They certainly have not released any information to the public."

Bolser stepped away to take a phone call.

The President turned to his Chief of Staff. "What's the casualty count from last night?"

Kingman tapped his PIB and fingered through some documents. "Meredith, New Hampshire was the hardest hit, three dead and twenty-three hospitalized. Hanover County, Virginia had two deaths and nineteen hospitalized. Rockland, Maine had two and fourteen. We don't have solid numbers, but we can assume there were a lot of other injuries that did not require hospitalization."

"And the injuries were mostly burns, correct?" asked Martin.

"Facial burns and eye injuries," said Kingman. "Apparently a lot people were blinded."

General Bolser returned to the table. "It looks as if we might have caught a break. Suspicious materials have been found in the unused fireworks from two communities that cancelled displays last night, one in Jefferson, Iowa, and the other in Fountain Valley, Colorado. We have teams en route now."

Thirty minutes later, the President entered a crowded White House press briefing room.

"Good morning. We apologize for the early briefing time, but we wanted to update you on what we know about last night's incidents in Virginia, New Hampshire and Maine.

"This morning, our thoughts and prayers are with the families of the seven people who were killed as a result of explosions during three different firework displays. We also send our best wishes to the fifty-six people that were hospitalized and many others who were also injured.

"Because of the highly unusual, yet similar, nature of these incidents, we are certain that they are related. I learned just minutes ago that two additional sites, one in Iowa and one in Colorado, were likely intended to be included in this coordinated attack.

"Personnel from the Federal Bureau of Investigations and the Bureau of Alcohol, Tobacco, Firearms and Explosives are working with local law enforcement at all five sites. Make no mistake, those responsible for these attacks will be identified and held accountable.

"I would also like to address the speculative comments that have appeared in various media this morning. There is absolutely no evidence supporting the claim that last night's incidents originated with the Hecatians.

"These are stressful times. It is understandable that people are searching for answers. Still, we must resist the urge to come to conclusions without solid evidence. To do so accomplishes nothing other than creating undo fear and panic.

"We will provide additional updates as new information is confirmed. Thank you." Martin left the podium without accepting questions. He did not have capacity for any more questions. What he needed was answers.

CHAPTER 56

Monday, June 29, 2037
The White House

President Martin found a rare, quiet moment as the cream swirled through his coffee. In stark contrast, Alan Kingman was wearing a path across the Oval Office rug.

They were waiting for General Bolser. The Secretary of Defense was on his way to the White House to brief the President on the results of the ongoing investigations surrounding the weekend incidents.

Despite the President's pleading for calm and patience, the media had continued to report even the most ridiculous theories related to the fireworks disasters. One news source had interviewed a former MIT professor who explained how the Hecatians used a cloaking device to mask their spacecraft while they hovered above the fireworks displays, firing death rays at the spectators.

General Bolser entered the room.

"Tell me you have something more believable than a cloaking device, General," said Martin.

"I do, Mr. President," said Bolser, taking a seat on the sofa. "We have completed our initial interviews with the fireworks vendors from each site. In all cases, these were small local companies that handle the procurement, delivery, setup and operation of the displays. We found no connection between these vendors, except for the fact that they all bought fireworks from the same manufacturer."

Kingman stopped pacing. "What are the odds of that?"

"There are just a few fireworks manufactures in the U.S., but they focus on the major displays for the big cities," said Bolser. "The small town shows tend to go for the cheaper stuff that is produced overseas. In this case, the manufacture was Flaming Dragon Fireworks which is located in Macau, China."

"No," said the President. "Not China."

"I'm afraid so, sir," said Bolser.

"The media will have a field day with this if it gets out," said Martin.

Kingman scanned the Internet on his PIB. "Too late, they already have it."

"I'm not surprised," said Bolser. "Reporters were all over the vendors as soon as we were done with them."

"Any chance this was deliberate on the part of the Chinese?" asked the President.

"At this point, I would have to say that it is possible," said Bolser. "The flash bombs were wired directly into the firework's cylinders. That would require familiarity with the pyro techniques and access."

"What do you mean by flash bomb?" asked Martin.

"The unspent devices that were found in Iowa and Colorado are an odd combination of argon and phosphorous," explained Bolser. "Argon ignites with a very bright light; easily bright enough to blind anyone nearby if they look directly at the explosion. But argon dissipates quickly. The phosphorous burns slower and would compound the effects of the argon, especially in the eyes."

"Has China used this type of device as a weapon before?" asked Kingman.

"Not that I'm aware of," said Bolser. "The combination is unstable and heavy. You would need a lot of both materials to have any kind of useful impact."

"They seemed to be pretty effective this weekend," said Martin.

"That's just it," said Bolser. "In the three incidents from Saturday night, the flash bomb exploded early in the trajectory. Six of the seven fatalities were actually members of the teams that were launching the fireworks. Most of the injured spectators were located close to the launch platforms as well."

Martin blew out a long breath. "So what does all this tell us, General?"

"We don't think the fireworks manufacturer would have integrated this device. They would have known that the rocket was not strong enough to carry the ordinate to altitude."

"But you said planting the devices would require familiarity and access," said Martin.

"That's right," said Bolser. "The military would have that kind of expertise."

"What about access?" asked Kingman.

"At some point, these fireworks would have been on a cargo ship," said Bolser. "What we don't know is if they were already allocated to a specific destination, or if they were shipped in bulk."

"For the moment, let's say this was a deliberate act on the part of the Chinese military," said Martin. "What would their objective be?"

Pings sounded, and all three men's PIB devices glowed.

"We might have that answer," said Kingman. "China just launched the spacedrone."

CHAPTER 57

Tuesday, June 30, 2037
The White House

I'm spending way too much time with you two," said the President as he entered the room.

General Bolser and Alan Kingman had been watching the morning press briefing from the relative calm of the Oval Office.

"We can wait, if you need more time with the media," said Kingman.

Martin smirked. "That was brutal. How many different ways can they ask me the same question?"

Expectedly, the focus of the press conference had been China. Was China responsible for the firework attacks? Did China launch the spacedrone to divert attention from the firework attacks? How was the U.S. planning to respond to the Chinese fireworks attacks and the Chinese spacedrone launch?

The President found it difficult to answer these questions because, over the last two days, every potential answer turned into another stack of questions.

"You guys have to give me something solid to work with," said Martin.

Bolser motioned toward something he was viewing from his PIB. "The Hecatians are tracking the spacedrone."

"How do we know that?" asked Martin.

"It showed up on the grey screen that tracks our orbit and the asteroid path," said Bolser. "We have created a secure link to the grey screen to make it easier for multiple people to monitor. You should see a new icon on your PIB's main page. We used the strophalos symbol."

Martin activated his PIB and tapped the icon. A holographic image of the Hecatian grey screen was displayed. Earth and the sun were prominent at the top and bottom of the screen. 29075 DA was just inside the arc representing Earth's orbit, about halfway between the planet and the sun.

"I assume this small mark just below the Earth is the spacedrone," said Martin.

"That is correct," said Bolser. "With magnification we can confirm that it is moving. The speed and direction matches the drone's flight path."

Martin nodded. "Any change on our estimated time of arrival?"

"No," said the General. "We still think it will catch-up to the asteroid sometime on Sunday. Premier Feng just released a statement referencing the same ETA."

"And here we thought we had cancelled all of the Fourth of July fireworks," said Kingman.

Gwen Hardin entered the room. "I'm sorry to interrupt, Mr. President, but we have an unusual situation that I'm not sure how to handle."

"What is it, Gwen?" Martin was concerned because this was the first time he had ever known Gwen not to be able to handle something.

"General Knudsen is at the west security gate. He is asking to see you. He says it is extremely urgent. I told him you were unavailable, but he said that was unacceptable. He says he has critical information that you must hear."

Kingman bolted from his chair and headed for the door. "I'll take care of this."

"Maybe it would be better if I handled it, Mr. Kingman," said Bolser, moving quickly to intercept the bulldog.

"Good idea, General," said Martin.

Kingman froze in place. His face was red and his heartbeat was visible from a vein in his neck.

"What could Knudsen possibly want to tell us, that we would want to hear?" asked Kingman as he loosened his tie.

"Probably nothing," said Martin. "But if he doesn't get to say it to us, he will likely say it to a television camera instead. Nothing good would come from that."

Kingman took a deep breath. "Good point."

Martin refocused on the grey sheet display. "I wonder if Feng plans to fly the drone directly into the asteroid."

"He's been pretty tight-lipped about that," said Kingman, returning to his seat. "I would be surprised if they try to do anything fancy."

The men spent the next few minutes in silence. Kingman's face had returned to the proper color and he seemed more at ease, until General Bolser returned to the room with Wilbert Knudsen behind him.

"Mr. President, I think we need to hear what General Knudsen has to say," said Bolser.

"Very well," said Martin.

"Thank you, Mr. President," said Knudsen. "I am certain that China had nothing to do with the firework attacks."

"You are already on record saying it was the Hecatians," said Kingman, shooting daggers toward Knudsen.

Knudsen raised a hand. "Please, just hear me out."

"Go on, General," said Martin, casting a calming look toward Kingman.

"When I entered the military, at turn of the century, my first assignment was with Weapons Research. One of the projects I worked on was an enemy deterrence ordnance that used a combination of argon and phosphorous to first stun, and then blind, enemy troops."

"General Bolser, didn't you say that you had never heard of this type of weapon?" asked Martin.

Bolser nodded.

"That's because the project was scrapped," said Knudsen. "It didn't have enough range to meet the objective. The deployment had to be perfectly targeted to be effective. Even then, it only affected people within a radius of a few hundred feet."

"That's consistent with what happened this weekend," said Martin. "Most of the people who were killed or injured were positioned very close to the fireworks launching areas."

"We had more success with targeted audio waves and laser-guided projects," said Knudsen. "The argon-phosphorous project was completely abandoned in 2008."

"What happened to the unused flash bombs?" asked Bolser.

"Due to the volatility of the argon, it was not safe to dismantle the bombs," said Knudsen. "They were turned over to a civilian contractor who hauled them to a secure site and detonated them."

General Bolser retrieved a photograph from his PIB. "Does this look familiar?"

Knudsen's eyes widened. "That's it! That is an argon flash bomb."

"We confirmed that Flaming Dragon Fireworks ships all of their product in bulk to a distribution warehouse in Los Angeles," said Bolser. "It's a massive building near the port that handles the brunt of the import business from China."

"That means the flash bombs would have to have been added after they arrived in the United States," said Kingman.

"We need to find out more about that warehouse and how the shipping, out of the warehouse, is handled," said Bolser.

Martin tapped his PIB. "Gwen, can you track down Aaron Ash?"

"I sure can," said Gwen. "He's standing next to my desk."

The Chief Butler entered the Oval Office looking like a teenager who had just been summoned to the principal's office.

"Mr. Ash," said Martin. "I understand you have several contacts in the global shipping arena."

"Yes, Mr. President, I have made quite a few acquaintances in that area over the years," said Ash, looking less nervous.

"We need to talk to someone who understands the logistics of the Chinese import business," said Bolser. "Things like overseas transport, warehousing, and distribution within the United States."

Ash smiled. "I know just the person. He spent decades in the import/export business before he joined the Federal Trade Commission. He's retired now, but he still owns a few shipping companies. In fact, one of his companies delivered your desk a few months ago, Mr. President."

"How fast can you get him here?" asked Martin.

"He still lives in D.C.," said Ash. "I should be able to get him here tomorrow."

"Perfect," said Martin. "Work with Gwen on the specifics. What is his name?"

"His name is Rudolph Overton."

CHAPTER 58

Tuesday, June 30, 2037
Washington, D.C.

He had always feared that, despite years of dreaming, decades of planning, and a lifetime of patience, his chance at redemption might still elude him.

For countless years, he had planted the seeds and cultivated the relationships. Ever vigilant to the simplest request, never shying when asked to do the impossible.

Today, his reward came in the form of a simple phone call. A request to, once again, share his knowledge and expertise. A summons to the palace, to stare into the eyes of evil, to exact his revenge, and deliver ultimate justice.

Rudolph Overton sat in stunned disbelief, teetering between elation and exasperation. He dare not even blink for fear that he would wake from this sweet dream.

Slowly he reached for his box and his key. It would be one last moment with his most precious possession, one last chance to buoy his determination.

A tear streaked his cheek when he replaced the item and closed the lid. He turned the lock for the final time, knowing that he would never come to this place again.

CHAPTER 59

Wednesday, July 1, 2037
The White House

Rudolph Overton ran a long finger across the side of the desk. "It truly is a work of art. I do so appreciate the chance to see it."

Aaron Ash beamed. "It's the least I could do after you worked that miracle to get it here so quickly."

Overton waived his hand. "Always willing to help a friend, and of course, my President."

As if on cue, President Martin entered the Oval Office, followed by Alan Kingman.

"Good morning Mr. Ash," said Martin.

"Good morning, sir. May I present Rudolph Overton."

Martin shook hands with his lanky visitor. "Pleased to meet you, Mr. Overton. Thank you for coming to the White House. This is my Chief of Staff, Alan Kingman."

"Mr. President, Mr. Kingman, I welcome the opportunity," said Overton, with a polite nod.

"I understand you played a key role in bringing this beautiful piece of furniture to its new home. I appreciate that."

"I merely made a few a phone calls, Mr. President," said Overton. "I was happy to help."

Mr. Ash exited, as the other men worked their way to the center of the room.

"The last time I was here, I believe there was a fireplace on that wall," said Overton.

"Yes, my predecessor had it removed," said Martin, glancing at the closet door. "Too bad, I think I might have enjoyed it."

They sat, Kingman on the sofa, the President in the adjoining chair. Overton sat in a chair at the opposite end of the coffee table. He opened a notebook and removed a pen from his shirt pocket.

"We understand that you have some expertise in the area of Chinese imports," said Kingman, "specifically, shipping and distribution."

Overton nodded. "It's been some years ago, but yes, I dabbled a bit in those waters."

"We think that some fireworks, imported from China, were tampered with after they arrived in the U.S.," said Martin. "We believe that flash bombs were added to some of the launch cylinders after they were designated for specific locations. Those were the bombs that were detonated this weekend."

Overton nodded calmly. "I understand."

"We are hoping that you could tell us if it would be possible for someone to infiltrate that warehouse and plant those devices," said Kingman.

"It might be possible to do that," said Overton. "But it would be easier to access the fireworks after they were loaded onto the delivery trucks."

Both Kingman and the President looked surprised. Apparently, they had found the right resource.

"It would?" asked Kingman.

"Yes," said Overton. "We use a large semi to pick up the fireworks from the import warehouse. We then load the orders for specific locations into delivery trucks at our own distribution center."

The look on Martin's face changed from surprised to confused. "Mr. Overton, you said we?"

"That's correct, Mr. President. I own the shipping company that delivered the fireworks."

The surprised look returned to the President's face. He looked at Kingman who was also obviously perplexed.

"I would not expect you to know that," Overton continued. "I leave the day-to-day operations to my staff. I am very hands-off."

Kingman moved closer to the edge of the sofa. "So you have already determined that the shipments were tampered with while they were on your trucks?"

"Yes," said Overton. "I have known that for some time."

"How did you know this?" asked Martin.

Overton grinned. "Because I orchestrated the whole thing."

Martin and Kingman sat in stunned silence.

Kingman inched closer to the sofa's edge; any closer and he would fall off. "Are you saying that you placed the flash bombs in the fireworks?"

"Not personally," said Overton. "A member of my staff did it for me."

President Martin was quickly losing his patience. "Mr. Overton is this some kind of sick joke?"

Overton shook his head. "I am not one that is given to nonsense, Mr. President."

"Where did you get the flash bombs?" asked Kingman

"From our warehouse," said Overton.

"You just happened to have a stack of argon-phosphate flash bombs sitting around your warehouse?" asked Kingman with no effort to mask his doubt.

"Yes," said Overton. "They had been there for twenty-five years."

Martin stiffened as he remembered General Knudsen's comments from the day before. "You were the civilian contractor that disposed of the excess flash bombs."

"That's correct," said Overton. "We detonated most of them. But I had my staff stash a few in the warehouse. I thought they might be useful at some point."

"Assuming this is all true," said Martin. "Why would you do this? Why would you hurt all those people?"

Overton's eyes narrowed. "I did not do this to hurt people. I did this to free people."

"Free people from what?" asked Kingman.

"From a government that operates in the shadows with lies and deceit," said Overton. "From people like you."

"You are out of line," said Martin.

"No!" shouted Overton. "You are out of line. Just like everyone who sat in this office before you was out of line."

"And you think killing and blinding a bunch of innocent people is going to correct these wrongdoings?" asked Martin.

Overton's pale face began to show a tint of pink. He pointed his pen at the President. "Killing people like you will stop the wrongdoings."

Kingman sprang to his feet. "You are going to sit here in the Oval Office and threaten the President of the United States? You are certifiably crazy."

"Sit down, Alan," said Martin.

Kingman returned to the sofa, never taking his eyes off Overton.

"Mr. Overton, I think it would be best if we concluded this conversation," said Martin. "You should speak to your attorney before we go any further."

Overton smirked. "I do not need an attorney. Attorneys are for people with something to hide. I have nothing to hide. But what about you, Mr. President? What are you hiding? How many attorneys work for you?"

Martin stood up. "We are done here."

As Overton rose from the chair, his pen fell to the floor. He bent down on one knee and reached beneath the coffee table, placing a hand on the tabletop to steady himself as he stood.

"No, we are very much not done here," said Overton. He calmly pointed a snub-nosed revolver directly at the President.

CHAPTER 60

Wednesday, July 1, 2037
The White House

The first thing President Martin noticed was how oddly calm the man holding the gun appeared to be.

"Do you like it?" asked Overton, with a slight nod toward the gun. "It's a 38 Special. Manufactured in 1947. Most appropriate, don't you think?"

Kingman rose slowly and stepped closer to the President, careful to keep his hands in sight. "That's impossible. You had to pass through at least two metal detectors when you entered this building."

Overton switched his stare to Kingman, but kept the revolver aimed at the President. "Mr. Kingman, why do you continue to doubt me?"

"Because, Yancy would have stopped you," said Kingman.

Overton squinted slightly. "Who is Yancy?"

"Oh, I forgot," said Kingman, speaking slowly and deliberately. "You don't know...Yancy!"

With a sudden burst, Kingman turned, swung his arm around the President's back, and fell to the floor in a heap behind the sofa. Two deafening shots rang out.

Overton coolly moved behind the sofa and stepped forward. He fired three times directly into the middle of Kingman's back. The President's body was completely covered by Kingman, except for his head, which was fully exposed. Overton moved slightly to his right and fired his last bullet into Martin's temple.

Doors on both sides of the office burst open and armed men streamed into the room. In an instant, Overton was pinned to the floor.

The last gun burst was still echoing in Martin's ear as he felt Kingman shifting on top of him. He felt several hands grabbing and twisting him onto his back. When he looked up he was face-to-face with Kingman.

"Are you OK?" said Kingman. Martin could barely hear, but he could read his lips.

"Are…you… OK?" Kingman repeated.

Martin took a deep breath. "Get off me."

One secret service agent helped Kingman to his feet, while Chris Boone assisted the President. Kingman immediately made a beeline for his assailant.

"I don't care how old you are, you sorry bag of bones. I'm gonna snap you in half."

The three agents who had tackled Overton had handcuffed him and lifted him to his feet. They formed a human shield around their prisoner. Overton barely registered Kingman's threat. He was staring at the gun on the floor.

Milford Townsend stepped forward and waited for Overton to look him in the eye.

"You're looking for these?" Townsend extended his hand, which was holding six bullets. "You were shooting blanks."

Overton looked bewildered as he stared at the bullets and then the coffee table. "But…"

"Would someone please tell me what hell is going on here," said Martin.

"Shortly after your desk was delivered, Mr. Townsend discovered a gun attached to the bottom of the coffee table," said Boone. "We questioned the two men who delivered the desk. One of them admitted to placing the gun. He said he was paid a great deal of money by an anonymous contact."

"OK. But why didn't you tell me about it?" asked Martin. "And why did you put the gun back under the table?"

"We needed to find out who was behind the threat," said Boone.

"I understand that," said Martin. "But who gave you the authority to do this without my knowledge?"

There was movement from the other side of the room.

"Mr. President, let me present the most tenured member of the Secret Service," Boone said, motioning with his arm.

The President gasped. "Townsend?"

"Yes, sir." Townsend moved closer to Martin. "We knew you would be safe because we replaced the bullets with blanks. We needed your reaction to be authentic. It was important that the would-be assassin follow through with his threat."

Martin ran his fingers through his hair as he processed what Townsend was telling him.

"But you clean this office every night. You're here at all hours of the day."

"That is my cover, Mr. President. But my primary objective is your safety, as it was for those who came before you, all the way back to your grandfather."

"Did my grandfather know that you were working for the Secret Service?"

"No, sir. This is the first time I have been exposed."

Martin walked to his desk. "Are there any other surprises that I should know about? Are there more guns hidden in my office?"

"No, sir," said Townsend.

"Knives?" asked Martin.

"No, sir," said Townsend.

"Cross-bows, nun-chucks, killer bunnies?" said Kingman, reducing the stress level in the room by several notches.

Overton was led from the room. Boone and the rest of the agents followed.

Townsend turned to the Chief of Staff. "Mr. Kingman, that was one of the bravest things I have ever witnessed."

"No kidding," said Martin. "What was that about?"

213

Kingman's look turned serious. "I knew from looking in that maniac's eyes that he was going to start shooting. I thought maybe I could keep him from getting both of us."

Rae Martin ran into the room. Relief washed over her when she saw her husband. After hugging him for several seconds, her mood shifted.

"Someone was shooting at you, in the Oval Office?"

"No," said Martin, searching for the right words.

"Don't lie to me James Martin," Rae demanded. "I heard gunshots all the way in the East Wing,"

"OK, yes," said Martin, "but they were blanks. I was never in danger."

Still red-faced, Rae turned to Kingman. "Alan?"

"He was never in danger, Rae," said Kingman. "It was just a scare, a big scare."

CHAPTER 61

Wednesday, July 1, 2037
The White House

R ae Martin clicked off the television and placed the remote on the bedside table.

"I should have known that the only thing on television would be detailed coverage of the one event I would most like to forget about," said Rae. "I can't believe you had to stand in front of the press and answer questions just hours after some madman tried to kill you in your own office."

James squeezed Rae's hand. "It was important to show the public that I was unharmed. People are pretty antsy right now."

"I know the feeling," said Rae. "And I know it had to be done, but some of those questions were ridiculous."

"No kidding," said James. "What was I thinking when the gun was pointed at me? What's the correct presidential response to that question?"

Rae was quiet for a long moment.

"What *were* you thinking?" she asked.

James thought. "First, I wondered how this guy could be so emotionless. Then I thought about you, which calmed me a little. Next thing I knew, Alan was on top of me."

Rae sat up in the bed. "You mean Alan protected you?"

"Yes. He threw me behind the sofa and covered me with his body."

"I must have missed that part of the press conference," said Rae.

"Alan was adamant that we not release those details."

"I don't care if they were blanks, he's a hero," said Rae.

"Absolutely," said James. "But if he wants to be a quiet hero, we will respect that, at least for the time being."

Rae kissed her husband and then burrowed into the blankets. James continued to read memos on his PIB.

After a few minutes, Rae reemerged. "Who is this Overton guy?"

"We still don't know a lot about him. He was a big-wig at the FTC for decades. Before that he was in the global and domestic shipping business. He's a bit of a recluse, never married. He grew up in New Mexico."

"Do you think he did all of this because of the Hecatians?" asked Rae.

"He made a point of telling us that his gun was made in 1947. That makes me think this has something to do with Roswell. The FBI and Secret Service are tearing apart his house. Hopefully that will tell us something."

James fingered through his PIB until he reached the strophalos icon. He swiped the image and brought up the grey sheet feed.

"What's that?" asked Rae, moving closer.

"It's one of General Bolser's new toys. This is the Hecatian grey sheet. They are tracking the spacedrone."

James adjusted the image so his wife could get a better look. "This is the sun. This is the asteroid. This is the Earth. This is the spacedrone."

Rae pointed to the screen. "What are these little triangles next to the asteroid?"

James checked the screen.

"Oh no," he said, bolting out of bed and fumbling for the phone icon. He raced to the closet to grab a pair of pants. "Alan, I need you and Bolser in the Situation Room immediately. We've got another problem."

CHAPTER 62

Thursday, July 2, 2037
The White House

It was just past midnight when General Bolser and Alan Kingman arrived at the Situation Room.

The President had already instructed the communication technician to route the grey screen feed to the main monitor in the middle of the room.

Bolser was the first to speak. "We've confirmed from the Hecatian's asteroid model that two ships have left the asteroid. It's a reasonable assumption that the triangles are those ships."

"That's what I was afraid of," said Martin.

"Can we tell where they are heading?" asked Kingman.

"It is certain they are heading toward us," said Bolser. "We will need a little more data before we can tell if they are on course for the drone or Earth."

"They are really moving fast," said Martin. "You usually can't see motion without magnifying the grey screen."

Kingman moved closer to the video screen on the wall. "Any way to estimate their speed?"

General Bolser shook his head. "We should be able to calculate that soon. But it is obvious they are moving faster than the asteroid and the drone."

Just as Bolser finished his comment, both triangles disappeared from the screen.

Kingman looked at Martin. Martin looked at Bolser. All three men then looked back at the screen. Seconds later, the triangles reappeared. They were now very close to the spacedrone, and they were no longer moving.

"Worm hole," said the President.

"Must be," said Bolser. "I have completely lost all perception of distance, but they had to have just traveled at least a few million miles."

"I thought worm holes only existed near the outer edge of our solar system," said Kingman.

Bolser leaned back in his chair, abandoning his ever-present military rigidity. "I'm beginning to question everything we think we know. None of this makes any sense."

There was a flicker of static on the screen. The display vibrated as if it were being affected by some type of electrical interference.

Martin turned toward the communication technician.

"That's not coming from our equipment," said the tech. "I see the same thing on our direct feed from the grey screen."

After a moment the display returned to normal. The triangles had not moved. The mark representing the drone was gone.

Kingman broke the silence. "Did they just destroy the spacedrone?"

"We have no way to easily verify that," said Bolser. "But that would be my guess."

President Martin rubbed his eyes. "You would think that staring down the barrel of a revolver would be the most unnerving thing that I would see in one day. But I'm not that lucky."

CHAPTER 63

President Martin sat at his desk in the Oval Office sipping on his third cup of coffee.

His head hurt from too little sleep. His back hurt, presumably from his wrestling match with YAK the day before.

Gwen Hardin tapped on the door. "Secretary Turner is here."

Martin just nodded.

Jordyn Turner took her place in front of the President's desk.

"Respectfully, Mr. President, you look horrible."

Martin managed a smile. "It's already been a long day. Please tell me you found someone in China willing to talk to us."

"Apparently the most populous country on the planet has gone completely mute," said Turner. "However, I have reliable sources in South Korea who tell me they have intercepted military communications from China confirming that the spacedrone was destroyed."

"Did these communications indicate how the drone was destroyed?"

"They did not, Mr. President," said Turner.

"I wonder if Premier Feng would like to reconsider his refusal of our offer to provide him with a link to the Hecatian tracking screen," said Martin.

"Probably not," said Turner. "He seems to be most happy when he is ensconced in ignorance."

The President finished his coffee. "Now that someone broke his favorite toy, perhaps he will play nice."

"We can always hope, sir."

As Secretary Turner left the office, Gwen entered with Chris Boone in tow. The agent was carrying a wooden box.

"Mr. President, can we fit in a few minutes with Mr. Boone before you head to the Capitol?"

"Ms. Hardin, if you say I have a few minutes, I have a few minutes," said Martin, motioning Boone toward the sofa.

Boone sat the box on the coffee table and took a seat across from the President.

Martin leaned forward and ran a hand underneath the top of the table. "Just checking," he said with a wink.

The agent smiled. "I deserve that, Mr. President, very funny."

"You and your team did a great job yesterday Agent Boone. Instead of ripping into you and Mr. Townsend, I should have thanked you."

"Your reaction was justified, Mr. President. There was a great deal of emotion in the room."

"Yes, there was," said Martin. "There was even more emotion in the residence last night. Still, thank you."

Boone nodded. "You're welcome."

"Tell me what you've learned about Rudolph Overton."

"Quite a bit," said Boone. "We kept him awake pretty late last night."

"Good. Was he in a talkative mood?"

"Most definitely," said Boone. "He repeated what he told you and the Chief of Staff about his role in the fireworks incidents. His story checks-out. He owns the shipping company. We also found two more flash bombs in his distribution warehouse. We are rounding up his employees so we can figure out who else needs to be charged."

"Any evidence that he was planning more attacks?" asked Martin.

"Not future attacks. But he did admit to involvement in another crime."

Martin leaned forward. "What crime is that?"

"The murder of President Rosemont."

Martin's eyes widened. "Really?"

"Yes. He also owns the shipping company that handles special projects for the Federal government, the same company that brought in your desk and planted the gun. They also managed President Rosemont's personal relocation to Key West."

"Are you saying one of his shipping employees killed Rosemont?"

Boone nodded. "That's what Overton told us. He was pretty smug about it. He said his man walked right into Rosemont's house, shot him in the chest, planted the evidence, and was on a boat to Barbados before anyone knew what happened."

"How does he get these people to do all these horrible things on his behalf?"

"Money," said Boone. "Apparently he paid very well."

"Does his Rosemont story hold water?"

"Yes it does. When we searched his house, we found a lot of evidence that he has been obsessed with the Roswell mysteries for decades. The most compelling evidence was in this box."

The President reached forward to examine the box. "What did you find?"

"We found a Hecatian grey screen. Just like those at Majestic. I gave it to General Bolser for authentication, but it sure looked like the real deal to me."

Martin was stunned. "So, Overton does have a connection to Roswell."

"He grew up in that part of New Mexico," said Boone.

Martin thought for a moment. "What did he tell you about his parents?"

"That was the only time he clammed up," said Boone. "He just said he barely knew his parents."

The President checked the wall clock.

"One more thing, Mr. President," said Boone, as he opened the wooden box. "There was one other item in the box with the grey screen. General Bolser said you would probably recognize it."

Martin pulled the box closer and looked inside.

His face went white.

He tapped the phone icon on the coffee table glasstop. "Gwen, I won't be going to the Capitol."

Boone looked at the President with concern. "Are you OK, sir?"

"I need you to take me someplace Agent Boone. You're not going to like it, but we're going nonetheless."

CHAPTER 64

Thursday, July 2, 2037
Arlington, Virginia

Rudolph Overton sat in an uncomfortable plastic chair in the middle of a small cinderblock room. His feet were shackled to the floor. His hands were shackled to the table in front of him. A florescent light hummed overhead.

Overton was wearing a threadbare orange jumpsuit that was at least two sizes too big for him. His new moniker, FEDERAL PRISONER, appeared in faded black across his back. He wondered how many deviants had worn this particular costume before him. Because of the smell, he also wondered if it had ever been laundered.

There was an empty chair on the other side of the table. Overton assumed it would soon be occupied by yet another investigator, who would ask the same questions that were asked a dozen times yesterday. He knew this was standard practice, but felt it was unnecessary because he had been entirely forthcoming.

The sound of keys rattling accompanied a commotion outside of the room. The door opened and Chris Boone stepped inside.

"Ah, Agent Boone," said Overton. "Are you here to ask me my name again?"

Boone paused. "No. I'm finished with you. There's someone else here who has a few questions."

He stepped aside and President James Martin entered the room, carrying a wooden box. Martin locked his eyes on Overton. Overton locked his eyes on the box.

Martin placed the box on the table and sat down. "Agent Boone, would you give us some privacy?"

Boone left the room.

The two men sat in silence. After a few moments, Overton shifted his focus from the box, to his visitor.

"Would you mind opening it for me?" said Overton, shifting his hand shackles.

Martin let the question hang in the air. "I'll open it, if you answer a question."

Overton gave a slight nod.

"What was your childhood like?"

The old man shifted his gaze to the side, as if he were searching for the words to a song that he had heard many years ago. "My childhood was lonely, and short-lived."

Martin opened the box. Overton leaned forward and let out a breath.

"I will remove it from the box, if you answer another question."

Overton whispered, "Yes."

"What were your parents like?"

Overton winced. His eyes grew moist.

"I never knew my mother. She died when I was very young. In a way, my father died with her."

Martin removed a pair of silver-framed cat-eye spectacles from the box. Each lens had a small spider-web crack. He closed the box and placed the spectacles on the lid.

Tears ran down Overton's cheeks.

"Please let me hold them," his voice barely audible.

"I will, if you tell me more," said Martin.

Overton closed his eyes tightly, squeezing out more tears.

"All I know is that she worked at the air force base. My father said she was a nurse. He said one day, some men came to the house and said she had died in an accident. They would not say how."

Overton swallowed hard, regaining some strength in his voice.

"A few days later, the men came back and gave my father her eyeglasses and some money. They said we could not have her body. They went through the house and took all of her pictures."

He paused and looked up at Martin, sobbing. "Why would they take the pictures? I don't even know what my mother looked like. Why would they take the pictures?"

Martin felt a lump in his throat. "I don't know."

Overton took another deep breath. "My father never got over it. He always talked about the UFO that had crashed a couple of days before the accident. He would go out to the crash site at night with a flashlight. He would bring home pieces of metal and put them in the box with the eyeglasses."

Martin picked up the eyeglasses and gave them to Overton. He held them gently, running a finger across the top of the frame.

"After he found the metal sheet with the glowing screen, he knew that he was right about the UFO. He stopped going to the crash site. He spent all of his time drinking and looking at the metal screen. I was seven years old when he died. When the social worker came to get me, she packed all of my clothes in a small suitcase. She said I could bring my favorite toy, but since I didn't have any toys, I took the box."

Martin searched for some way to console the man who had sought to kill him the day before.

"I lost my mother not too long ago," he said.

The old man gave the President a chilling look.

"Don't you dare," said Overton. "You had a lifetime with your mother. You have a grave to visit. You have memories. I have nothing, Mr. President. This country, that you hold so dear, took everything I had."

Martin sat quietly for a moment, and then he stood and left the room, leaving the eyeglasses and the box behind.

CHAPTER 65

Saturday, July 4, 2037
The White House

President Martin and Alan Kingman stood on the Truman Balcony watching the fireworks display on the skyboard across the lawn.

The President's executive order banning fireworks was still in effect. In lieu of the traditional public celebrations, patriotic music videos had been playing on skyboards across the nation all day. After nightfall, the broadcasts switched to videos of fireworks.

"This has to be the most pathetic thing I've ever seen," said Kingman.

Martin burst into laughter. "It is pretty bad."

"Reminds me of the holographic Christmas tree app that I have on my PIB," said Kingman.

The laughter continued as Rae entered the balcony.

"I thought you would like to know that the steaks are almost ready," she said. "What are you two up to out here?"

"Just enjoying the show," said Martin.

Rae watched the display for a few moments. "They should have stuck with the music videos."

Kingman nodded in agreement. "Next year, things will be back to normal. We can have twice as many fireworks."

"That would be nice," said Rae, slipping an arm around her husband. "I'd better get back downstairs, our guests are waiting."

Martin kissed his wife. "We'll be right down."

On her way out, Rae gave Kingman a big hug and a peck on the cheek. "Thank you, Alan."

Kingman blushed. "What did I do?"

"You know what you did," said Rae, slipping through the door.

Kingman looked at Martin. "Really, what did I do?"

"It doesn't matter that they were blanks, Alan," said Martin.

"Don't start that again," said Kingman. "It was no big deal."

"It is a big deal. How many people in the world actually find out that someone cares enough to take a bullet for them?"

Kingman rolled his eyes. "You would do it for me too."

"I would. But that's beside the point. The point is, I want to thank you for being here with me. Not just with the shooting, but this whole alien mess. There are a lot of great people working with us. But if it weren't for you and Rae, I couldn't do this."

Rather than his usual flippant retort, Kingman opted for the less comfortable sincere response. "I do this because I believe in you, James. You're the only person I know who could handle this. Just keep going, we're almost there."

"Thanks," said Martin.

"Don't mention it. Now, can I please have that steak?"

CHAPTER 66

Monday, July 6, 2037
The White House

Gwen Hardin stood beside the President's desk as Martin reviewed his schedule for the week.

"You were not joking when you said things were really starting to pile up," said Martin.

Gwen shook her head. "No, sir, and there are a couple dozen meetings that I have yet to fit on the schedule."

"We can do some evening meetings this week," said Martin. "And if anyone is willing to meet me at 5 a.m., I'll be here."

Gwen raised an eyebrow.

"That doesn't mean *you* have to be here," said Martin. "I'm perfectly capable of unlocking the door."

"Very well," said Gwen, heading for her office.

"Who is first today," asked Martin.

"Aaron Ash. You won't like it."

Ash entered the office.

"Good morning, Mr. Ash," said Martin. "How was your weekend?"

"It was fine. Thank you, Mr. President."

Ash stood in front of Martin's desk, looking uncertain.

"What can I do for you, Mr. Ash?"

Ash took a breath. "Mr. President, first I want to apologize for what happened last week. It was my poor judgment that allowed Rudolph Overton to gain access to this office."

Ash handed the President an envelope. "Secondly, I would like to tender my resignation."

Martin tapped the envelope on the desk as he considered the Chief Butler's comments.

"Have you found another job, Mr. Ash?"

"No, sir, I have not."

"Are you unhappy in your current position?"

"No. I love what I do, Mr. President."

The President handed the unopened envelope back to Ash.

"Mr. Ash, Rudolph Overton is, by far, the saddest individual I have ever met. I doubt the man has ever enjoyed a day of happiness. He is also a brilliant man, who manipulated people for decades. I don't hold you at all responsible for anything that man did."

Ash bowed slightly. "Very well then. Thank you, Mr. President."

Martin watched as Ash left the room and Craig Bolser entered.

"General, are you coming to upset my schedule?"

"Just some news from China, Mr. President. Their state-run media is reporting that they have moved another spacedrone onto the launch site."

Martin shook his head in disbelief. "This Feng guy has no quit in him."

"Apparently not," said Bolser. His comment was interrupted by someone banging on the window.

The President and Bolser both moved toward the window overlooking the Rose Garden. Alan Kingman was pointing upward. The normally peaceful garden was filled with Secret Service agents and White House staff. Everyone was looking at a nearby skyboard.

The board displayed a large gunmetal grey strophalos. The curving maze and center spiral glowed in purple.

Martin turned toward Bolser who was already on the phone.

Alan Kingman entered the office.

"That just popped up about three minutes ago," said Kingman. "Sounds like every skyboard in D.C. is displaying the same thing."

Bolser lowered his phone. "We are getting reports from all over the globe. Everyone is seeing the strophalos. We are trying to reach the skyboard operations center to find out where it's coming from."

The President rejoined Kingman at the window as the General moved to the other end of the office. "It's either the world's greatest hacker, or the Hecatians."

"That's kind of eerie," said Kingman. "It's like they're marking their territory."

More of the staff was starting to come out into the Rose Garden. They gathered, two or three to a group, and talked as they gazed upward. Fear was a common feature on every face.

Just then, the skyboard display changed, further agitating the crowd. The strophalos was gone, replaced with two side-by-side pictures. The first was of a spacedrone in flight. The second was a photo of Earth from space. A large red X appeared over the planet.

"Not gonna happen," the President said to himself.

"What was that?" asked Kingman.

Martin shook his head. "Nothing. I was just thinking that they are speaking our language."

Bolser joined them at the window.

"The skyboard people say they have totally lost control of the system," said Bolser, looking up at the new display. "They have no idea who or what is controlling it."

"I think it's pretty obvious who's controlling it," said Kingman.

"I agree," said Martin. "And the message is clear, launch another drone and it will be the last thing we do."

Bolser was still staring at the skyboard. "What do we do next, Mr. President?"

"We get Premier Feng on the phone," said Martin.

CHAPTER 67

Monday, July 6, 2037
The White House

The Situation Room buzzed with activity.
President Martin, General Bolser and Alan Kingman were seated at the conference table. The skyboard display, still showing the Hecatian message, was on one video screen. A live shot of the second Chinese spacedrone was on another screen, courtesy of a military satellite.

This particular satellite was one of General Bolser's newest toys. It could read the VIN number through the windshield of any car. More impressively, it could put a laser-guided missile through the sunroof.

The President checked the wall clock. It was just past noon. "General Bolser, if we don't hear from Feng in the next hour, take out the drone."

Bolser nodded.

Jordyn Turner, and her diplomatic staff, had been working from the State Department all morning, trying to get Premier Feng to agree to a phone call. A videoconference line from the Secretary of State's office had been left open so Turner could provide updates every fifteen minutes.

Turner appeared on screen.

"I think we are getting close, Mr. President. Several of the United Nation's highest ranking officials have been calling Feng on our behalf. They have urged him to speak with you before launching another drone."

"He's got less than an hour," said the President. "I'm tired of messing around with this guy."

"I understand," said Turner. "I'll be back as soon as I hear something."

Kingman started pacing around the table. "If we fire on that drone, while it's still on Chinese soil, it's an act of war."

Martin nodded. "True. But if that drone launches, the Hecatians will consider it an act of war. I'd rather take my chances with China."

Kingman and Bolser both agreed.

A few minutes later, a communications technician announced that a call was coming in, just as Secretary Turner appeared on the videoconference screen.

"That's him," said Turner.

Martin looked at the technician, "Speaker phone."

Premier Feng could be heard speaking Mandarin in the background. After a few seconds, the translator's voice joined in.

"It is very late and I am very busy, President Martin. What do you want?"

"I want to know what you are planning to do with that spacedrone."

"I am planning to launch it, obviously."

"They destroyed your last drone, Premier Fang. How will this one be any different?"

"The first drone had a mechanical failure. The aliens had nothing to do with it."

"I watched them blow up your drone myself," said Martin

"You are lying."

"I know the skyboards in your country are displaying the same Hecatian warning that we are seeing. Are you just going to ignore that?"

"That is just more American propaganda," said Feng. "Everyone knows that you control those skyboards."

Martin ran his fingers through his hair and took in a deep breath.

"Let me state this another way, Premier Feng. You will remove that drone from the launch tower in the next hour, or I will remove it myself."

"You should be sure your sabre is sharp before you rattle it, President Martin."

Feng disconnected the call.

The President turned to General Bolser.

"How long until they could launch that drone?"

Bolser's normally emotionless face showed concern. "It is already fueled and armed. A nighttime launch is not ideal, but they could do it."

"Take it out now," said Martin.

"Sir?" asked Bolser.

"We're not waiting. Blow it up."

Bolser swiveled in his chair and tapped his PIB.

"We have another phone call, sir. From the same number as before," said the tech.

"Hold on, General," said Martin.

The tech activated the speaker phone.

"Mr. Feng, I think we have said everything we need to say to each other."

A man, different from Feng, spoke slowly in English.

"President Martin, this is Vice Premier Chen. Premier Feng has been relieved of his duties. I am now in charge. We are making preparations to remove the spacedrone from the launch site."

Kingman pointed to one of the video screens on the wall. A large crane could be seen moving toward the launch tower.

"That is welcome news, Mr. Chen. Thank you."

"I would like to take steps to restore diplomatic activities between our countries. Many here agree that we should have a unified global front when dealing with the Hecatians."

"I'm very glad to hear that," said the President. "Our Secretary of State will contact you soon."

233

Martin disconnected the call.

Kingman fell into his chair. "I don't know how much more of this I can take. One minute, we're on the brink of war, the next, we're playing nice."

"With Feng out of the picture, things should calm down a bit," said Bolser.

Martin pointed to the screen that was monitoring the skyboard. The display had switched back to the grey and purple strophalos.

"I agree, General," said Martin. "It should be calmer, at least until next month."

CHAPTER 68

President Martin was seated on the sofa in the Oval Office. For the first time in weeks he was genuinely pleased with the information he was hearing. Finally, something was progressing as planned.

Not surprisingly, it was the project that Rae was leading.

The first lady and Dennis Gordon had spent the last ten minutes briefing the President on the current status of the gas-mask project. The numbers were encouraging, 85% of the masks were manufactured and 40% were already delivered.

"Everyone on the planet will have a mask by the end of the month," said Gordon.

Martin stood and shook Dr. Gordon's hand. "This is great news. I hope you will pass along my thanks to your team."

"I will, Mr. President," said Gordon as he headed for the door.

"And you, Mrs. Martin," said the President, reaching for his wife with both hands and kissing her lightly. "Congrats. This is quite an accomplishment."

Rae beamed. "Thanks, but Dr. Gordon and the Red Cross team deserve all the credit."

As the couple walked toward the President's desk, General Bolser entered the room.

"Don't be a stick-in-the-mud, General," said Martin. "I'm feeling really good right now."

Bolser's face remained stoic. "Sorry, sir, but you need to check the Hecatian's tracking sheet."

Martin tapped his PIB. Rae started to leave.

"You might as well see this now, ma'am," said Bolser. "It will be common knowledge soon."

The President enlarged the holographic image and positioned it so Rae and the General could see it.

"Oh my goodness," said Rae.

"Is this all of them, General?" asked Martin.

"Yes," said Bolser. "The asteroid is completely empty. They launched about 15 minutes ago."

The tracking sheet showed 29075 DA, which was now well inside Earth's orbital path. Several clusters made up of small triangles were moving away from the asteroid.

"How many ships?" asked Martin.

"Thirty-two," said Bolser.

Martin switched off his PIB and sat at his desk.

"I thought we had until August," said Martin.

Bolser nodded. "We have all been working with that assumption, since that is when the asteroid will be closest to Earth."

"How long do we have?" asked Martin.

"A few days," said Bolser. "Less if they find another worm hole."

"We will be lucky to have half of the gas-masks distributed by then," said Rae.

"Our only hope is that they like our alternate habitation plan," said Martin. "How far along is the relocation of the residents near Ayers Rock and the Canada-Montana site?"

"It started last week," said Bolser. "We can speed that up."

The President looked at his wife. "Let's focus the mask distribution in the areas surrounding those sites."

Rae nodded.

"Anything else, Mr. President?" asked Bolser.

Martin thought for a long moment.

"I don't know what it would be, General. I'm completely out of ideas."

CHAPTER 69

Thursday, July 9, 2037
The White House

President Martin had a habit of cutting through the public area of the White House, on his way to the West Wing, at least once a week. This gave him a chance to interact spontaneously with members of the public who were taking the guided tour.

The Secret Service obliged the President in this matter because the White House was the most secure building on the planet, despite anything that Rudolph Overton would say.

It always caused quite a commotion in the crowd when the President rounded the corner. The tour guide would always say the same thing. "Here's a special treat ladies and gentlemen, the President of the United States."

Martin did this, not because it made him feel special, but because it made the people feel special.

Despite yesterday's events, today was no different.

Cameras clicked, people reached to shake his hand, a few asked for autographs, and some simply said hello.

As was his custom, the President always sought out the smallest child in the room. He would joke with them for a few moments and then present them with a special gift.

The President spotted a small boy hiding behind his mother. He shook the woman's hand.

"And who do we have here?"

"This is Alex," she said. "He doesn't usually act like this. He's very outgoing."

Martin peeked at the boy and smiled. "Hi there, Alex."

Alex tried to disappear behind his mother.

Martin got down on one knee so he was eye-to-eye with the boy. "Are you shy?"

Alex shook his head.

"Are you scared?"

Alex nodded.

"Are you scared of me?"

Alex shook his head.

"What are you scared of, Alex?"

Alex reached into his mother's tote bag and removed a magazine. On the cover was a picture of a flaming strophalos looming over the Earth, along with the words END OF THE WORLD in bold print.

"You're scared of the aliens?"

Alex nodded.

"Can you tell me why you're afraid of the aliens?"

Alex moved closer to the President. "They are going to come here and hurt us."

Martin took ahold of the boy's hand. "They are not going to hurt us, Alex."

"How do you know?" asked Alex.

"Alex, how old are you?"

"Six."

"When I was six, I wanted to be an astronaut."

Alex brightened. "I want to be an astronaut too."

"If you were an astronaut, would you want to visit other planets?"

Alex nodded enthusiastically.

"And if you visited other planets, would you want to meet the people who lived there?"

More nodding.

"Alex, if you visited another planet, and met the people who lived there, would you want to hurt them?"

"No," said Alex. "I would be nice to them."

Martin smiled. "That's how I know that the aliens are not going to hurt us."

The President retrieved a small teddy bear from his jacket pocket. The bear was wearing a blue shirt imprinted with the presidential seal.

"I found this little guy in my office the other day. Do you think you could give him a good home?"

"Sure I can," said Alex, grabbing the bear.

"Thanks, buddy," said Martin, as he tousled the boy's hair. "Do you feel better now?"

"Yeah," said Alex, cuddling the bear.

"I'm glad to hear that," said Martin, as he stood up.

Alex's mother had tears in her eyes. "Thank you. Thank you so much."

As the President hugged the boy's mother, he noticed that several other people standing nearby were also misty-eyed.

"We're going to be OK folks," said Martin. "Keep the faith."

CHAPTER 70

Thursday, July 9, 2037
The White House

President Martin entered the Oval Office and immediately checked the tracking sheet on his PIB.

The Hecatian ships were about halfway between the asteroid and Earth.

Martin headed for the closet door. Without hesitation, he moved past the flag stands and into the living room.

Mortimer and Emma were standing in the middle of the room, as if they had been waiting for his arrival. The room seemed brighter; not as brown. The fireplace still crackled, but the flame was not as dull. The puppercat was nowhere in sight.

"Mr. President," said Mortimer, with his familiar bow.

"Hello, Mortimer. Emma," said Martin.

"The days are growing more challenging," said Mortimer. Emma nodded.

"That they are," said Martin. "People are terrified."

"People often find the unknown terrifying," said Mortimer. "But were it not for the unknown, we would not need leaders like you."

"But I'm scared, too," said Martin.

"There is nothing wrong with being scared, Mr. President," said Mortimer.

"Morty's scared to death of spiders," blurted Emma. "That's unfortunate when you live inside a wall."

Martin smiled. "Emma, if you don't mind, I really need to focus here."

Emma's eyes danced with delight. She stepped forward and patted the President on the back. "You're going to be fine, Jimmy."

Martin watched as Emma quietly left the room. He then turned his focus back to Mortimer, who was beaming like a proud father at a Little League game.

"Was it something I said?" asked Martin.

"It was less about what you said, and more about what you thought," said Mortimer. "You have learned to cut out the clutter. You have learned to keep your mind focused on what's important."

Martin paused. "So, I won't be seeing Emma anymore?"

"Like me, Emma will always be around in one way or another," said Mortimer. "You may see us again, or you may not. Seeing us is not important. What is important is what you have come to realize, and accept, deep inside of you."

"But I still don't know if you are real, Mortimer," said Martin.

Mortimer bowed slightly, and blinked slowly, just as he had done the first time they had met. "I will tell you what I have told those who came before you. It does not matter if the ghost you see in the hall is real. It does not matter if the cat you see in the basement is real. It does not matter if the voices that come to you in your dreams are real. It does not matter if your dog really talks back to you. It does not matter if the couple under the desk, or inside the closet, is real. What matters is what is left in your heart after you consider the message."

"But what if I do everything that a leader is supposed to do, and I'm still wrong?" asked Martin.

"If you are wrong, you will deal with it," said Mortimer. "That is what leaders do."

Mortimer took the President's hand. "See it through, James. See it through."

CHAPTER 71

Thursday, July 9, 2037
The White House

James and Rae Martin sat quietly on the comfy sofa in the White House residence. They had long-since turned off the television, having grown weary of doomsday pronouncements.

They had spent the last half-hour talking by phone with Deanna and Paul. James was pleased to learn that they had decided to spend the next few days with Dad. Deanna was excited because he was having a rare good day. He was not his old self, but he was clearer and more talkative.

James was waiting for Deanna to put their dad on the phone.

"Hello, pup," said Joe Martin.

James immediately started to cry. Rae took his hand.

"Hey, Dad, it's good to hear your voice. I understand you have some company."

"Yes, Deanna and Paul are here," said Joe. "But your mom's not. She died, James."

James swallowed hard. Rae squeezed his hand.

"I know, Dad. I'm really sorry about that. I sure miss her."

"I miss her, too," said Joe.

As had been the case the last few times that he talked with his dad, James did not know what to say.

"What do you think about these aliens, James?" asked Joe.

"Well, that's the big question of the day."

"Are they going to hurt us?" asked Joe.

James wiped at his eyes.

"They are not going to hurt us. We're going to be fine."

"That's good," said Joe.

"I'm going to come see you in a couple weeks," said James. "How does that sound."

"That would be good. But mom's not here."

"That's OK. I would just like to see you."

"OK," said Joe.

"I love you, Dad."

"Love you too, James."

James disconnected the call and buried his face in Rae's shoulder. He stayed there for several minutes trying to regain his composure.

"You handled that very well, sweetheart," said Rae.

James held his wife.

"I just hope I didn't lie to him."

CHAPTER 72

Friday, July 10, 2037
The White House

President Martin stood on the patio overlooking the south lawn of the White House. He had watched many helicopters land from this vantage point over the last six months. Today he watched as a different type of aircraft moved through the sky.

Thirty-two aircraft, to be exact.

Martin had received word from General Bolser, shortly after 9 a.m. that the Hecatian ships had passed through a worm hole and emerged between Earth and the moon.

By noon, the spacecraft had entered Earth's atmosphere, high above Europe. The hope was that they would split into two groups and navigate to Australia and Southern Canada. That did not happen. Instead, the full contingent crossed the Atlantic Ocean and was now in formation over Washington, D.C.

The skyboards, which had resumed normal operation after the Chinese spacedrone was removed from the launch tower, were again displaying the strophalos.

Rae had joined him on the patio, as had General Bolser and Alan Kingman. After a half-hearted attempt to convince the President to move to a more secure location, Chris Boone had taken a position just outside the door to the patio.

Martin had given all of the staff approval to leave the White House and join their families. Several had departed, but many remained, and were gathered on the lawn. Gwen Hardin and Aaron Ash stood together in the middle of the crowd.

The largest Hecatian craft had moved to the front of the formation and was hovering a few hundred feet above the lawn.

The skyboard flickered and Martin reached for his wife's hand. The image of an alien head came into focus. Martin recalled the corpse that he had viewed at the Pentagon. He was again mesmerized by the alien's inky black eyes.

Beings of Earth. We are from the world that you have called Hecate.

The alien's eyes pulsated rhythmically with each syllable. Though the alien's mouth did not move, Martin clearly heard each word, but not in the normal fashion. He heard the words in his head, soft, clear and somehow comforting.

He turned slightly toward Rae. "Are you hearing this?"

"Yes," she whispered. "It's strange. I hear both English and French."

Martin turned back to the skyboard and was again drawn into the eyes of the Hecatian.

Our world is no more.

We have searched the stars for a new world to sustain us. Long ago, we found your world, glistening across the cosmos. It was well-suited to our needs.

But now, your world has grown ill. The air is unclean and the sun shield has grown thin. What once glistened is now dim.

Your offer to share a piece of your world warms us. Yet we will search for a healthy world to sustain us perpetually, rather than a fleeting respite.

We wish for you to learn from our world, one that we presumed would heal itself and endure, despite our depredation. We do not want the people of your world to suffer the same fate.

We gift you with knowledge from our world.

We wish peace and wellbeing for your world.

CHAPTER 73

Friday, July 10, 2037
The White House

President Martin sat in the Oval Office with Alan Kingman and the first lady. General Bolser had stepped away to take a phone call from the Majestic team.

The trio was still reveling in the relief generated by the alien address. The crowd on the South Lawn had erupted in cheers as the Hecatian contingent departed. President Martin and Rae had embraced and thanked each and every staff member as they reentered the building.

"That was the strangest thing I've ever experienced," said Kingman. "It was like he was in my brain, controlling my thoughts."

"She," said Rae.

Both Kingman and Martin turned to the first lady.

Rae smiled. "I definitely heard a woman's voice in my head."

"Seriously?" asked Kingman.

Rae nodded.

"Now that's freaky," said Kingman. "How did they do that?"

"I have a feeling we are several thousand years from understanding that technology," said Martin. "Right now, I'm more interested in knowing what they meant by gifting us with knowledge from their world."

"Maybe they consider warning us that our planet is unhealthy, and in danger, to be a gift," said Rae.

"Perhaps," said Martin. "And if that prompts us to stop ignoring the issue, like we have for the last 50-plus years, it would be a gift."

General Bolser entered the room with a serious look on his face.

The President held up his hand and shook his head. "General, I swear, if you are bringing me more bad news, I'm going to give your job back to Knudsen."

Bolser grinned, ever so slightly. "I do not have bad news, Mr. President. But I do have news from the team at the Pentagon."

"Let's hear it," said Martin.

"The three alien bodies, which were housed at Majestic, are gone."

The General paused for comments, but his audience just looked confused.

"When Dr. Gordon returned to his lab, after listening to the Hecatian address, the aliens were missing."

"They took their fallen comrades with them," said Martin. "That should not surprise us."

"There is more," said Bolser. "When Dr. Lindsey returned to her warehouse, she had a surprise as well."

"Did they take their crashed spacecraft too?" asked Kingman, with a hint of disappointment.

"No," said Bolser. "They rebuilt it. All of the separate pieces of the craft had been moved to the center of the warehouse and completely reassembled."

"That's the gift," said Rae.

Bolser nodded. "It gets better. NASA has been receiving files from the Hecatians for the last hour. The files are in the same formats as the files that we sent to them as part of Project Dove. The files contain detailed instructions on how to construct the small spacecraft and the larger transporters. They also explain the chemical makeup of the weightless material."

President Martin stood and walked toward his desk.

"General, as soon as we have this information organized, we need to immediately share all of it with Japan and China and every other country on Earth that has a space program."

"Absolutely," said Bolser.

"Why would they give us this information?" asked Kingman. "Do they want us to be able to join them in their space explorations?"

"I think that is part of it," said Bolser. "But in addition, just as they did for themselves, I think they want to ensure that we can protect humanity if we ever need to escape this planet."

"You are correct, General," said Martin. "And our top priority needs to be making sure that we never need to escape this planet."

EPILOGUE

James Martin surveyed the Oval Office from the center of the room. Some things had changed; new paint, new drapes, and different artwork. The Resolute Desk was back. Still, despite the cosmetic differences, the aura of the room was the same as it had been for the eight years that he had called it home.

"Mr. President, I'm so sorry to keep you waiting," said the current occupant of the office, while hurrying into the room and grasping Martin's hand. "Please sit. Thank you so much for meeting with me."

Martin sat on the sofa. It, too, was new, softer, but still appropriately elegant. A silver coffee service sat on the table in front of the sofa. "It's my pleasure. I like what you've done with the place."

There was a light knock on the side door. A tall, fit, black man, dressed in a suit and tie, entered the room. Martin caught the young man's eyes as he handed the current President an envelope.

"Have we met?" asked Martin.

The man smiled broadly. "No, sir, but I believe you know my grandfather."

"Townsend!" exclaimed Martin, rising to shake the man's hand. "I should have known that from the start."

"Yes, sir," said the man excitedly. "I'm Russell Townsend. Gramps sends his best."

Martin beamed. "Well, you tell him I said hello and that I hope he is enjoying retirement. Looks like your family is going to keep an eye on this office for a while longer."

"At least for a while," said Russell, turning his attention to the new President. "I sure appreciate the opportunity."

"It was an obvious choice," said the President, pouring coffee into three cups. "Russell is my top administrative aide, fresh out of NYU."

The three sat and shared stories about Russell's family and their various connections to the White House. Martin noticed that all three added cream to their coffee, Russell stirred, while the two Presidents inconspicuously glanced at the swirls in their cups.

After a while, Russell excused himself, leaving the Presidents alone to conduct their business.

"So, Madame President," said Martin. "What can I help you with?"

President Jordyn Turner shifted slightly in her chair. "I need to ask you some personal questions, if you don't mind?"

"Go ahead," said Martin.

President Turner paused for a moment, and then leaned forward toward Martin, "I'd like you tell me everything you know about hawks."

At that instant, President James Patrick Martin was certain that, somewhere in the distance, he could hear a fireplace crackle.

A Special Request

Congrats! You made it through the story. You outlasted Overton. You survived the Hecatians. You finally figured out Mortimer (or maybe not).

Did you enjoy the book? Did it end the way you hoped? Do you have questions or suggestions? I would really like to hear from you. Please take a moment to send me an email at awilson1414@gmail.com. Thank you.

Anthony Wilson

About the Author and the Story

Anthony Wilson traces the initial inspiration for *Mortimer* back to a high school senior class trip to Washington, D.C. in 1984. As a journalist in the late 1980s, Anthony was encouraged to resist the urge to write a novel. As a parent in the 1990s, he did not have time to write a novel. As a project manager in the early 2000s, he was not sane enough to write a novel.

In 2007, Anthony rekindled the original spark and secretly started typing. What began as a study of leadership, morphed into a futuristic/sci-fi/fantasy with a thinly veiled message... you can handle whatever life throws at you as long as you trust in yourself, stay focused, and lean on your friends and loved ones.

Anthony has a bachelor's degree in Communications from Missouri Southern State University (Joplin, MO) and a master's degree in Human Resource Development from Pittsburg (KS) State University. He lives in Rochester, MN, with his wife, Linda.

CPSIA information can be obtained at www.ICGtesting.com
Printed in the USA
LVOW12s0746190813

348494LV00002B/8/P